Dirty Old Town

A Shane Cleary Mystery #1

Gabriel Valjan

DIRTY OLD TOWN

A Shane Cleary Mystery #1

LEVEL
BEST BOOKS

First published by Level Best Books January 14, 2020

First edition

ISBN: 978-1-9479-1544-2

This book was professionally typeset on Reedsy.
Find out more at reedsy.com

Contents

Praise for the Shane Cleary Mysteries

"Robert B. Parker would stand and cheer, and George V. Higgins would join the ovation. This is a terrific book—tough, smart, spare, and authentic. Gabriel Valjan is a true talent—impressive and skilled—providing knock-out prose, a fine-tuned sense of place and sleekly wry style." — Hank Phillippi Ryan, nationally bestselling author of *The Murder List.*

"Fans of Robert B. Parker's Spenser and Dennis Lehane's Patrick Kenzie will love Shane Cleary. Gabriel Valjan has created a fascinating new PI character who prowls the tough streets of '70s Boston in this compelling hard-boiled mystery. Dirty Old Townis fast, fun and first-rate!" — R.G. Belsky, author of the award-winning Clare Carlson mystery series.

"*Dirty Old Town* hits every pitch out of the park: it's smart, funny and consistently surprising. A great read!" — Dennis Palumbo, author of the Daniel Rinaldi Mysteries

"Say hello to Shane Cleary, a down-on-his luck private detective walking the streets of dirty old Boston, circa 1975. He's smart, sarcastic, and tough, despite a few cuts and bruises. And he's got a gift for describing everything he sees like a painter with a brush dipped in acid. So come for the twisting plot and suspense, stay for the style. Author Gabriel Valjan has done a terrific job bringing Shane and his world to life. You'll read it in one sitting." — William Martin, *New York Times* Bestselling Author of *Back Bay* and *Bound for Gold.*

"Valjan paints the town, and all the colors are noir." — Tom Straw, *New York*

v

Times Bestselling author, as Richard Castle.

The People

Shane Cleary: South End, Boston private investigator.
Delilah: Shane's cat.
Catherine Braddock: Wife of Brayton and Shane's ex-girlfriend.
Brayton Braddock: Husband of Catherine, and Shane's childhood friend.
Delano 'Professor' Lindsey: Shane's former teacher, mentor, and father figure.
Bill: Friend of Shane and an Army veteran.
Eddie: Former confidential informant and current owner of a coffee shop.
Jimmy C: Arsonist.
Nathaniel Dunbar: Auditor.
Roger Sherman: Friend of Bill's.
Marty Savitz: Sports agent.
John: Bar and pool hall owner, and husband of Sylvia.
Sylvia: Owner of Sister Sylvia's, a soul food restaurant in Dorchester, and John's wife.
The Barbarian: Hit man.
Mr. B: Mafia don.
Mr. Butch: Street entertainer, Kenmore Square.
Tony Two-Times: Bodyguard and associate of Mr. B.

Chapter 1: Bait

The phone rang. Not that I heard it at first, but Delilah, who was lying next to me, kicked me in the ribs. Good thing she did because a call, no matter what the hour, meant business, and my cat had a better sense of finances than I did. Rent was overdue on the apartment, and we were living out of my office in downtown Boston to avoid my landlord in the South End. The phone trilled.

Again, and again, it rang.

I staggered through the darkness to the desk and picked up the receiver. Out of spite I didn't say a word. I'd let the caller who'd ruined my sleep start the conversation.

"Mr. Shane Cleary?" a gruff voice asked.

"Maybe."

The obnoxious noise in my ear indicated the phone had been handed to someone else. The crusty voice was playing operator for the real boss.

"Shane, old pal. It's BB."

Dread as ancient as the schoolyard blues spread through me. Those familiar initials also made me think of monogrammed towels and cufflinks. I checked the clock.

"Brayton Braddock. Remember me?"

"It's two in the morning, Bray. What do you want?"

Calling him Bray was intended as a jab, to remind him his name was one syllable away from the sound of a jackass. BB was what he'd called himself when we were kids, because he thought it was cool. It wasn't. He thought it made him one of the guys. It didn't, but that didn't stop him. Money creates delusions. Old money guarantees them.

"I need your help."

"At this hour?"

"Don't be like that."

"What's this about, Bray?"

Delilah meowed at my feet and did figure eights around my legs. My gal was telling me I was dealing with a snake, and she preferred I didn't take the assignment, no matter how much it paid us. But how could I not listen to Brayton Braddock III? I needed the money. Delilah and I were both on a first-name basis with Charlie the Tuna, given the number of cans of Starkist around the office. Anyone who told you poverty was noble is a damn fool.

"I'd rather talk about this in person, Shane."

I fumbled for pen and paper.

"When and where?"

"Beacon Hill. My driver is on his way."

"But—"

I heard the click. I could've walked from my office to the Hill. I turned on the desk light and answered the worried eyes and mew. "Looks like we both might have some high-end kibble in our future, Dee."

She understood what I'd said. Her body bumped the side of my leg. She issued plaintive yelps of disapproval. The one opinion I wanted, from the female I trusted most, and she couldn't speak human.

I scraped my face smooth with a tired razor and threw on a clean dress shirt, blue, and slacks, dark and pressed. I might be poor, but my mother and then the military had taught me dignity and decency at all times. I dressed conservatively, never hip or loud. Another thing the Army taught me was not to stand out. Be the gray man in any group. It wasn't like Braddock and his milieu understood contemporary fashion, widespread collars, leisure suits, or platform shoes.

I choose not to wear a tie, just to offend his Brahmin sensibilities. Beacon Hill was where the Elites, the Movers and Shakers in Boston lived, as far back to the days of John Winthrop. At this hour, I expected Braddock in nothing

2

less than bespoke Parisian couture. I gave thought as to whether I should carry or not. I had enemies, and a .38 snub-nose under my left armpit was both insurance and deodorant.

Not knowing how long I'd be gone, I fortified Delilah with the canned stuff. She kept time better than any of the Bruins referees and there was always a present outside the penalty box when I ran overtime with her meals. I meted out extra portions of tuna and the last of the dry food for her.

I checked the window. A sleek Continental slid into place across the street. I admired the chauffeur's skill at mooring the leviathan. He flashed the headlights to announce his arrival. Impressed that he knew that I knew he was there, I said goodbye, locked and deadbolted the door for the walk down to Washington Street and the car.

Outside the air, severe and cold as the city's forefathers, slapped my cheeks numb. Stupid me had forgotten gloves. My fingers were almost blue. Good thing the car was yards away, idling, the exhaust rising behind it. I cupped my hands and blew hot air into them and crossed the street. I wouldn't dignify poor planning on my part with a sprint.

Minimal traffic. Not a word from him or me during the ride. Boston goes to sleep at 12:30 a.m. Public transit does its last call at that hour. Checkered hacks scavenge the streets for fares in the small hours before sunrise. The other side of the city comes alive then, before the rest of the town awakes, before whatever time Mr. Coffee hits the filter and grounds. While men and women who slept until an alarm clock sprung them forward into another day, another repeat of their daily routine, the sitcom of their lives, all for the hallelujah of a paycheck, another set of people moved, with their ties yanked down, shirts and skirts unbuttoned, and tails pulled up and out. The night life, the good life was on. The distinguished set in search of young flesh migrated to the Chess Room on the corner of Tremont and Boylston Streets, and a certain crowd shifted down to the Playland on Essex, where drag queens, truck drivers, and curious college boys mixed more than drinks.

The car was warmer than my office and the radio dialed to stultifying mood music. Light from one of the streetlamps revealed a business card on the seat next to me. I reviewed it: Braddock's card, the usual details on

3

the front, a phone number in ink. A man's handwriting on the back when I turned it over. I pocketed it.

All I saw in front of me from my angle in the backseat was a five-cornered hat, not unlike a policeman's cover, and a pair of black gloves on the wheel. On the occasion of a turn, I was given a profile. No matinee idol there and yet his face looked as familiar as the character actor whose name escapes you. I'd say he was mid-thirties, about my height, which is a liar's hair under six-foot, and the spread of his shoulders hinted at a hundred-eighty pounds, which made me feel self-conscious and underfed because I'm a hundred-sixty in shoes.

He eased the car to a halt, pushed a button, and the bolt on my door shot upright. Job or no job, I never believed any man was another man's servant. I thanked him and I watched the head nod.

Outside on the pavement, the cold air knifed my lungs. A light turned on. The glow invited me to consider the flight of stairs with no railing. Even in their architecture, Boston's aristocracy reminded everyone that any form of ascent needed assistance.

A woman took my winter coat, and a butler said hello. I recognized his voice from the phone. He led and I followed. Wide shoulders and height were apparently in vogue because Braddock had chosen the best from the catalog for driver and butler. I knew the etiquette that came with class distinction. I would not be announced, but merely allowed to slip in.

Logs in the fireplace crackled. Orange and red hues flickered against all the walls. Cozy and intimate for him, a room in hell for me. Braddock waited there, in his armchair, Hefner smoking jacket on. I hadn't seen the man in almost ten years, but I'll give credit where it's due. His parents had done their bit after my mother's death before foster care swallowed me up. Not so much as a birthday or Christmas card from them or their son since then, and now their prince was calling on me.

Not yet thirty, Braddock manifested a decadence that came with wealth. A pronounced belly, round as a teapot, and when he stood up, I confronted an anemic face, thin lips, and a receding hairline. Middle-age, around the corner for him, suggested a bad toupee and a nubile mistress, if he didn't have one

4

already. He approached me and did a boxer's bob and weave. I sparred when I was younger. The things people remembered about you always surprised me. Stuck in the past, and yet Braddock had enough presence of mind to know my occupation and drop the proverbial dime to call me.

"Still got that devastating left hook?" he asked.

"I might."

"I appreciate your coming on short notice." He indicated a chair, but I declined. "I have a situation," he said. He pointed to a decanter of brandy. "Like some...Henri IV Heritage, aged in oak for a century."

He headed for the small bar to pour me some of his precious Heritage. His drink sat on a small table next to his chair. The decanter waited for him on a liquor caddy with a glass counter and a rotary phone. I reacquainted myself with the room and décor.

I had forgotten how high the ceilings were in these brownstones. The only warm thing in the room was the fire. The heating bill here alone would've surpassed the mortgage payment my parents used to pay on our place. The marble, white as it was, was sepulchral. Two nude caryatids for the columns in the fireplace had their eyes closed. The Axminster carpet underfoot, likely an heirloom from one of Cromwell's cohorts in the family tree, displayed a graphic hunting scene.

I took one look at the decanter, saw all the studded diamonds, and knew Elizabeth Taylor and Richard Burton would have done the set number of paces with a pair of hand-wrought dueling pistols to own it. Bray handed me a snifter of brandy and resumed his place in his chair. I placed my drink on the mantel. "Tell me more about this situation you have."

"Quite simple, really. Someone in my company is blackmailing me."

"And which company is that?"

"Immaterial at the moment. Please do take a seat."

I declined his attempt at schmooze. This wasn't social. This was business.

"If you know who it is," I said, "and you want something done about it, I'd recommend the chauffeur without reservation, or is it that you're not a hundred percent sure?"

I approached Bray and leaned down to talk right into his face. I did it out of spite. One of the lessons I'd learned is that the wealthy are an eccentric and paranoid crowd. Intimacy and germs rank high on their list of phobias.

"I'm confident I've got the right man." Brayton swallowed some of his expensive liquor.

"Then go to the police and set up a sting."

"I'd like to have you handle the matter for me."

"I'm not muscle, Brayton. Let's be clear about that. You mean to say a man of your position doesn't have any friends on the force to do your dirty work?"

"Like you have any friends there?"

I threw a hand onto each of the armrests and stared into his eyes. Any talk about the case that bounced me off the police force and into the poorhouse soured my disposition. I wanted the worm to squirm.

"Watch it, Bray. Old bones ought to stay buried. I can walk right out that door."

"That was uncalled for, and I'm sorry," he said. "This is a clean job."

Unexpected. The man apologized for the foul. I had thought the word "apology" had been crossed out in his family dictionary. I backed off and let him breathe and savor his brandy.

I needed the job. The money. I didn't trust Bray as a kid, nor the man the society pages said saved New England with his business deals and largesse.

"Let's talk about this blackmail then," I said. "Think one of your employees isn't happy with their Christmas bonus?"

He bolted upright from his armchair. "I treat my people well."

Sensitive, I thought and went to say something else, when I heard a sound behind me, and then I smelled her perfume. Jasmine, chased with the sweet burn of bourbon. I closed my eyes, and when I opened them I saw his smug face.

"You remember Cat, don't you?"

"How could I not?" I said and kissed the back of the hand offered to me. Cat always took matters one step forward. She kissed me on the cheek, close enough that I could feel her against me. She withdrew and her scent stuck to me. Cat was the kind of woman who did all the teaching and you were grateful for the lessons. Here we were, all these years later, the three of us in one room, in the middle of the night.

"Still enjoy those film noir movies?" she asked.

"Every chance I get."

"I'm glad you came at my husband's request."

The word husband hurt. I had read about their marriage in the paper.

"I think you should leave, dear, and let the men talk," her beloved said.

His choice of words amused me as much as it did her, from the look she gave me. I never would have called her "dear" in public or close quarters. You don't dismiss her, either.

"Oh please," she told her husband. "My sensibility isn't that delicate and it's not like I haven't heard business discussed. Shane understands confidentiality and discretion. You also forget a wife can't be forced to testify against her husband. Is this yours, Shane?" she asked about the snifter on the brandy on the mantel. I nodded. "I'll keep it warm for you."

She leaned against the mantel for warmth. She nosed the brandy and closed her eyes. When they opened, her lips parted in a sly smile, knowing her power. Firelight illuminated the length of her legs and my eyes traveled. Braddock noticed and he screwed himself into his chair and gave her a venomous look.

"Why the look, darling?" she said. "You know Shane and I have history."

Understatement. She raised the glass. Her lips touched the rim and she took the slightest sip. Our eyes met again and I wanted a cigarette, but I'd quit the habit. I relished the sight until Braddock broke the spell. He said, "I'm being blackmailed over a pending business deal."

"Blackmail implies dirty laundry you don't want aired," I said. "What kind of deal?"

"Nothing I thought was that important," he said.

"Somebody thinks otherwise."

"This acquisition does have certain aspects that, if exposed, would shift public opinion, even though it's completely aboveboard." Braddock sipped and stared at me while that expensive juice went down his throat.

"All legit, huh," I said. "Again, what kind of acquisition?"

"Real estate."

"The kind of deal where folks in this town receive an eviction notice?"

He didn't answer that. As a kid, I'd heard how folks in the West End were tossed out and the Bullfinch Triangle was razed to create Government Center, a modern and brutal Stonehenge, complete with tiered slabs of concrete and glass. Scollay Square disappeared overnight. Gone were the restaurants and the watering holes, the theaters where the Booth brothers performed, and burlesque and vaudeville coexisted. Given short notice, a nominal sum that was more symbolic than anything else, thousands of working-class families had to move or face the police who were as pleasant and diplomatic as the cops at the Chicago Democratic National Convention.

I didn't say I'd accept the job. I wanted Braddock to simmer and knew how to spike his temperature. I reclaimed my glass from Cat. She enjoyed that. "Pardon me," I said to her. "Not shy about sharing a glass, I hope."

"Not at all."

I let Bray Braddock cook. If he could afford to drink centennial grape juice then he could sustain my contempt. I gulped his cognac to show what a plebe I was, and handed the glass back to Cat with a wink. She walked to the bar and poured herself another splash, while I questioned my future employer. "Has this blackmailer made any demands? Asked for a sum?"

"None," Braddock answered.

"But he knows details about your acquisition?" I asked.

"He relayed a communication."

Braddock yelled out to his butler, who appeared faster than recruits I'd known in Basic Training. The man streamed into the room, gave Braddock two envelopes, and exited with an impressive gait. Braddock handed me one of the envelopes.

I opened it. I fished out a thick wad of paperwork. Photostats. Looking them over, I saw names and figures and dates. Accounting.

"Xeroxes," Braddock said. "They arrived in the mail."

"Copies? What, carbon copies aren't good enough for you?"

"We're beyond the days of the hand-cranked mimeograph machine, Shane. My partners and I have spared no expense to implement the latest technology in our offices."

I examined pages. "Explain to me in layman's terms what I'm looking at, the abridged version, or I'll be drinking more of your brandy."

The magisterial hand pointed to the decanter. "Help yourself."

"No thanks."

"Those copies are from a ledger for the proposed deal. Keep them. Knowledgeable eyes can connect names there to certain companies, to certain men, which in turn lead to friends in high places, and I think you can infer the rest. Nothing illegal, mind you, but you know how things get, if they find their way into the papers. Yellow journalism has never died out."

I pocketed the copies. "It didn't die out, on account of your people using it to underwrite the Spanish-American War. If what you have here is fair-and-square business, then your problem is public relations—a black eye the barbershops on Madison Ave can pretty up in the morning. I don't do PR, Mr. Braddock. What is it you think I can do for you?"

"Ascertain the identity of the blackmailer."

"Then you aren't certain of…never mind. And what do I do when I ascertain that identity?"

"Nothing. I'll do the rest."

"Coming from you, that worries me, seeing how your people have treated the peasants, historically speaking."

Brayton didn't say a word to that.

"And that other envelope in your lap?" I asked.

The balding halo on the top of his head revealed itself when he looked down at the envelope. Those sickly lips parted when he faced me. I knew I would hate the answer. Cat stood behind him. She glanced at me then at the figure of a dog chasing a rabbit on the carpet.

"Envelope contains the name of a lead, an address, and a generous advance. Cash."

Brayton tossed it my way. The envelope, fat as a fish, hit me. I caught it.

Chapter 2: Mushrooms

"Put it behind you." I heard those words at my father's funeral, the same words verbatim the umpteenth time after I pulled the zipper on a body bag in Vietnam, and from the little old ladies who volunteered at the VA, and again when Cat wrecked my existence and married Bray. Put it behind you, they all said.

History. Cat and I had it. Braddock and I shared her before she upended our lives, mine more than his, since he won and married her. We were only kids then. The Braddocks had taken me in for a short time, harbored me when I became a true orphan after my mother's death. Briefly.

Dad gone, and now mom, the Commonwealth of Massachusetts searched for relatives and found none, so I disappeared into foster care. I stayed on at St. Wystan's, either because the priests had pitied me or some mysterious benefactor out of a Dickens novel stepped up with the tuition so I could finish my secondary education. As for foster care, surrogate parents came and went; they changed as often as Boston's weather.

Hot. Cold. Indifferent. Unpredictable.

I endured, lashed myself to my studies, and whatever thought I might've had for higher education died with my parents. I chose the Green Machine, joined the United States Army before it had the chance to draft me. Until the day I left on a train for Georgia, the land that God forgot, where I swatted more flies and scraped more mud than I cared to remember, I remained, as Brother Ray said, sweet on the girl.

Cat then was pale, coltish, blonde, and in possession of a crooked smile and eyes that didn't give a damn what they liked. Her voice, close to you, on you, promised everything Lauren Bacall insinuated with an arched eyebrow. I had it, I had all that, and yet she picked Bray because she had a name and no money, and he had money and a name.

And that was how the song ended for me. No Shane and Cat sitting in a tree, K-I-S-S-I-N-G. No, first comes love, then marriage, then baby in a carriage for us. Nope. None of it.

I woke up after a short stint of shut-eye, convinced that bad karma was forcing me to deal with my unresolved issues with Mr. and Mrs. Brayton Braddock III.

I needed coffee better than the Folgers Instant in my office. Delilah insisted on lap time, which made a review of the photostats difficult. She kneaded my upper thigh. The way her eyes squinted and opened wide and her claws hooked into me said she had sensed another woman. "It's not what you think," I told her.

Bray had given me a name and place, but before proceeding, I wanted that coffee. I could use another opinion and I knew where to get it. These numbers added up right, cross-referenced each other, and matched what Braddock had said last night. However much I disliked the screw job, the Boston handshake on paper, it all smelled legit, fair-and-square and ship-shape on crinkly paper. And yet, nothing is that kosher outside of a deli. I placed Delilah in one of her favorite spots. I hid the bulk of the advance from Bray in my Boston Five account under a floorboard. I pocketed a decent amount for personal use.

December weather called me and I responded to it with a long coat and I remembered the gloves this time. No scarf—not after a suspect tried to strangle me once with one. I wore last night's shirt to enjoy Cat's scented imprint.

***

A hard wind cleaned out one of the side streets near South Station. A solitary page from a newspaper twirled like a tornado before a gust lifted it high up into the sky. I was cutting through the Leather District to South St., where I would find Lindsey in his usual seat at the diner watching the morning traffic on Atlantic Ave.

Delano Lindsey has been a regular since '47, the year it opened and I came into the world, unplanned like most kids. It was called The Blue Diner then. Open seven days a week, twenty-four hours a day, it fed tourists, A-listers from the Theatre District, dealers from Eastie, gun-runners for the IRA out of Brighton, and the usual business types from the burbs, who fled manicured lawns and the morning stare-down from the missus. He spotted me and waved from the back of the eatery.

Lindsey, formerly a professor at a certain red brick establishment in Cambridge, had fallen from grace after 'allegations of misconduct' with a student behind his desk, on the floor and after hours. The girl, who wasn't his student, said it was all consensual, not that it mattered. Lindsey claimed departmental politics and a vendetta. I could relate after my short stint with the Boston Police Department. I wanted to believe Lindsey, but, in my experience, the goat who thinks with his horn loses his place in the farmer's yard to the ax.

He was once upon a time my Latin and Literature instructor at St. Wystan's and, after I had left, he helped me, mind and body, with books and several Alexander Hamiltons inside as a bookmarker. Past fifty, no job and zilch for a pension, he hustled placement agencies for paying gigs. He gave me a brief hug and two hearty pats on the back. I peeled off my gloves.

"I need an opinion, Professor."

"Sit, and let's chat over coffee."

"Make it breakfast."

Before he could balk and claim he wasn't hungry, I flagged a waitress. I suspected the professor hadn't had a decent meal in days. He was often as hard up for money as I was, but I had some in my pocket, thanks to Brayton. I held up two fingers and pointed a finger to myself and Delano. Breakfast Special No. 2 for two. A nod of her head and she went to the window and placed our order with the cook in the pit.

The diner offered gastronomical courage for men and women charging the front lines of a dull day. Waffles with rigid squares held butter and syrup until the heel of a fork cleaved them in two. Bacon crunched. Coffee sang reveille and of love for duty. A standard favorite usurped every child's hatred

12

of Brussels sprouts. The cook would shred the sprouts, toss in bits of bacon and cubed potatoes, and crown the hash with a light poached egg that ran silky.

Our coffees arrived first.

"Brayton Braddock hired me. He says someone is blackmailing him."

He knew the name well, but glossed over it with his question. "Name of a suspect?"

"Some guy, an accountant, who roams around his companies. He would have his nose inside all of the books."

"Means established, but what about a motive?"

"With Brayton, you never know."

Always one sugar and a splash of half-and-half, the professor stirred his coffee, and I watched black turn to mocha. He had a book near the window. *Anna Karenina*.

"Bray's never been straight with me. Even since we were kids, there's always a twist with him. Why the hell should I trust him now?"

"Then why did you take the job?"

"Want of money."

"*Radix malorum est cupiditas*. The root of evil is greed."

Our plates of eggs, heaps of hash browns, and two strips of bacon and sides of toast arrived. My fork separated my browns. I lifted a mouthful. The professor broke an egg, slowly and deliberately. I could tell from his eyes that he was hungry. I've seen and known the look before. I've always wanted to ask but never did, whether he had any stock with the Delanos of Hyde Park, New York. His cadence of speech had the same pitch and intonation as FDR's. While we ate, I recapped what Brayton had said about acquisitions, how it was all legal, and how I thought he wanted damage control.

"Why would he lie?" Delano asked.

"Why wouldn't he? All I've got is his word. A blackmailer sends Xerox copies but doesn't attach a page from *The Herald* or something to suggest he'd leak it to the paper?"

The professor wiped his mouth with a napkin. "Did you say Xeroxes? Few offices in Boston have those machines." He rubbed his fingers together.

"Expensive. Let me have a look, please."

I crunched toast, reached into my pocket, and hand handed him the documents. He looked away when he saw the grip of the holstered .38 when my coat puckered. We'd had our debates over conceal-and-carry, and I knew he disapproved, but I felt safer with it in the South End and on the job.

I savored the next few bites of buttered bread and I poked my eggs. The yolks didn't run too fast, the potatoes were just right, and I've never argued with bacon. The professor thumbed through the papers. He held one page and then another up close to his eyes. He lifted his frames off his nose.

"Need better glasses?"

"My eyesight is fine. This is what bothers me."

He turned a page to face me. Now I was the one who had to squint. His finger tapped it. "That is on several pages in the exact same place."

"And?" I shrugged. "I don't know a thing about Xerox machines, other than I've heard that they make a racket." His fingernail traced what looked like a hairline fracture. "Look at it again, Shane."

I did. He showcased each page as if they were exhibits in a trial. I reconsidered the evidence. "Same location on each page, consistent looking. Same Xerox machine?"

"Exactly, and I know the machine."

"Where?"

I was curious if the professor's answer matched the address Bray had given me.

"Let's finish breakfast first."

He handed the copies back to me. We continued our meal. We had one of those miniature jukeboxes near us. A dial on the top animated a windmill of selections, all of them awful, although Simon & Garfunkel's "My Little Town," number eight on *The Pop Top 20* this week, reminded me of this dirty old town.

The sudden unexpected noise from a dropped plate turned me in my seat, a hand tight to the chest for my .38. I closed my eyes, inhaled and counted to five in my head.

"Still have those nightmares?" he asked.

14

"Not nightmares, Professor. I never liked sudden noises."

"Still think you should see someone, Shane."

"There's nothing to discuss."

I felt guilty, rude even. I wanted to apologize, but was too macho to do so. My silence would make it disappear. I heard the rhythmic sounds of a broom and shards swept into a pan. The waitress cleared our table and we ordered more coffee.

"It's a scratch on the drum inside the Xerox machine," Delano said. "Leaves a fingerprint on every page."

"In the exact spot?"

"Every time," he said.

I waited, while the waitress poured us more coffee, then asked, "Know where this magical drum lives?"

"Little Building, off the Common, near Chinatown. Third floor."

Name. Address. Brayton had told the truth, for once in his life.

"Off the Common," I said. More like a euphemism for the Combat Zone. I shook my head. "A real sewer."

I heard the clink of the spoon soon enough. The professor opened up his Tolstoy. I was certain the Little Building wasn't a Braddock property, which led me to think that a business associate of his owned it. Bray had given me the name Dunbar, said he was a consultant, so I had to determine whether this accountant was renegade help, or working at the behest of one of Bray's partners.

"Shane?"

"Yeah."

"You may need the money, but you went to see her, didn't you?" Lindsey used his finger to follow text in his Tolstoy. "That's the real reason, isn't it?"

"I need the money."

"But you knew she'd be there."

"Jobs have been scarce as water in the desert since the Douglas case went to trial, or have you forgotten?"

I knew he was listening. He waited, like a parent, for that moment when the child overcommits and compounds guilt with remorse. I fell into the trap

15

when I said, "I should never have talked to the DA. Don't say you disagree."

"I do disagree, my boy. You see yourself as a man who takes no side, but you did the right thing when you could have easily done the wrong thing, and nobody would've known."

Lindsey remained stoical, unmoved and still reading Tolstoy.

"Don't butter me up because I'm buying breakfast."

"It's not flattery. Your idealism, while admirable, is from a bygone era."

"I was fond of Marlowe when I was a kid."

"You're not a kid anymore," he said and reached to touch the top of my hand. "You exposed corruption and gave a black family a voice and some solace, Shane Cleary. I just wish you had exercised a little restraint. This is the real world, not a Chandler novel."

I loved Delano Lindsey. Like a father, I did, but the professor didn't know crap about the real world. He was learning hard lessons now, looking for a job after a life in the cloisters of academe. He simplified matters for one thing. Justice comes with a price. I lost my job, had to leave it, and probably would look over my shoulder for the rest of my life. What I admired about Ray Chandler's Marlowe was that he had a code. Cops do, too. It goes by many names.

Blue Line. Blue Wall. Blue Veil.

I had crossed it, smashed it, and pierced it when I testified that a beat cop had killed an unarmed black kid in a Southie project. Not my partner, not my case. It didn't matter. I had done the unthinkable, the unforgiveable. Some solace that kid's family received.

The cop lost his badge, his pension, and he pled out to the lesser charge of manslaughter, rather than chance it with a jury or bench verdict. The judge assigned the case wasn't on the payroll, or sympathetic. In this town, in this age, and with politics the way they were, I doubt a jury would've convicted Officer Douglas. With time served and good behavior, he'll get out on probation and it won't matter the color of the traffic light because the hearse was coming for me then, if not sooner. The professor understood some of that, sure, but he had no idea what it was like when someone wanted to kill you.

16

The cup hit the saucer with a loud *clink*. I hadn't realized he was deep in monologue.

"Splendid work you did, but next time exercise discernment."

"Discernment?" I mumbled.

"A knight on horseback has no chance galloping toward a machine-gun nest. Think of those poor bastards in World War I. Consider a better strategy next time."

Words of advice from a man who never saw combat.

"Thanks, but since the boys in blue have my name stitched into their hats, I'll likely be the first person in Boston shot for nonpayment of parking tickets, and I don't even own a car."

I raised my hand to signal for the check. I told the professor his money was no good. He insisted, argued that he'd at least pay for his coffee. He wanted to his maintain his dignity, so I accepted his pocket change. I could use it for phone calls. I calculated the bill, figuring in a nice tip, and jammed some folded bills into the professor's breast pocket. "Not a word," I told him and scanned the room for our waitress. "I'll be right back."

As I moved past him, he grabbed my arm. "What now?" I asked.

"Fuck'em. I mean it, Shane. You did the right thing, and I'm proud of you. Don't ever forget that." He released his grip on my arm.

I walked over to the register. Only two things I understood on the bill: the green and white rows for background and the sum. I heard the sharp ring of the bell, the cough of the cash drawer. Our waitress appeared, both hands full, so I dropped a Lincoln into her side pocket and thanked her. I returned to bid farewell to the professor.

"How's the job hunt?"

"Not enough experience, or I'm overqualified. Who wants to hire an old fart?" he said.

"I've got to get going, Professor."

"I was thinking about your situation."

"Not now, please," I said.

"Have you ever read *Anna Karenina*?"

"No, but the gist of it is avoid train tracks. I get it."

He pleaded that I listen to him. He handed me the book and pointed to a passage. I read a paragraph about some guy named Sergei Ivanovich and a woman named Varenka. Tolstoy was inside the head of two characters at once. These two were in love with each other, and both of them were together in the forest, picking mushrooms. He loves her but doesn't have the nerve to tell her. She loves him and hopes that he'll propose to her. Lindsey told me the outcome.

"You're kidding," I said. "Moment comes, and he asks her about the difference between two types of mushrooms?"

"It's a metaphor, Shane."

"Yeah, yeah, I get it, Professor. One lost moment and no marriage equals two mushrooms." I fixed my collar. "You forget, Cat is married."

He smiled.

"I'll stick to my 'avoid the train tracks' version. Thanks."

He smiled again.

"What is with you and the smile?"

He got up from his chair, cupped his hands around the back of my head and shook my skull. His eyes brightened and he was laughing the laugh you couldn't help but join, and then he said it, "This isn't about you and Cat.".

"What then?"

"Discernment, my boy. It pays to know the difference between mushrooms because the wrong one can kill you."

Chapter 3: A Fare to Pay

The professor's advice to see someone about my nightmares hurt me like a paper cut under the fingernail. The professor meant well. I tried to talk to a shrink, once—some jarhead with icy eyes and corn-fed features, straw for hair and about as much for brains or empathy. I talked and he listened, but it was all formality, because the brass wanted each guy separated from the service, cleaned—disinfected is more like it—of the 'Post-Vietnam experience.' Our chat was nothing more than a perfunctory exit-interview, a checkbox on a standard military form.

I knew Lindsey's counterargument. There were numerous social workers and psychiatrists in Boston, he'd say, those who could and would coax a veteran to that popular word these days: *closure*. I don't buy it. I don't think a civilian has the capacity to understand how the chatter of gunfire can rattle nerves, or how a breeze made you think of Death opening her wings before a firefight, or why a grunt would kill himself after receiving a Dear John letter from his girl back home. Those letters were hard on most men. At least a grenade whistled before the puff of smoke, the shrapnel.

The professor suggested a woman counselor. I had heard that women were storming the caring professions, while I was in-country and after I returned. Everyone pointed to Hot Lips on *M*A*S*H**. I had known nurses in Nam, and I respected those ladies. We respected the Red Cross volunteers, too. Every soldier also appreciated coffee and donuts, and none of us would disparage the women we called Donut Dollies, but we didn't share our terrors from our time in the fields with them. Men didn't do that.

Loco, my Portuguese amigo, told me once: 'Guilt will make you the Ancient

Mariner, and talk all you want, but the world will tell you that you never should've gone to sea. They'll never understand nor will they care.'

Last I heard from him was a letter with a picture of him in Lisbon, a sea of red carnations around him and 25 April 1974 was written on the back of the photograph. He was wearing smart jazzy clothes and a wide grin, but I saw him for what he had become—a man back from the dead, Lazarus with lifeless eyes.

I rucked with all these thoughts on Washington Street, my mind loaded with what the professor had said about the scratches from a Xerox machine, about them being unique as a fingerprint, and about the drum inside the Little Building. I attempted crossing Summer Street, only to have the short bleats of a cop's whistle disturb all that weight inside my head.

I clenched. I half-expected the report of my demise in tomorrow's *Boston Globe* to read **MAN KILLED WHILE RESISTING JAYWALKING TICKET**, the first in the history of the Commonwealth of Massachusetts. Dirty South Station and its green sign behind me, I did a slow turn, hands visible, and found my reflection in the mirrored sunglasses of a patrolman.

"Bill? Is that you?" I said, now aware of the cruiser behind him.

"Got a minute?"

Bill and I had served in the Army. We'd been two young kids who'd never known the other existed until we rode the bird home together. Bill served as the point man, the first man in a reconnaissance patrol. First to shoot or first to die. Point was to balls, what the rearmost guy with the M60 was to heart. Any guy in recon was thankful when either man sounded off.

"Don't think it's wise for you to be seen talking to me," I said.

Bill had taken the shades off. He knew I meant his partner in the patrol car parked at the curb, yards behind him. I looked to see whether the man radioed in my location. He hadn't. Bill did his impression of John Wayne, thumbs looped over his belt. "I've got a job for you. A possible missing persons case in Bay Village."

"Why don't you and your partner work it?"

Bill scratched his eyebrow. His said the case wasn't in the feeder, and his partner was coasting it into retirement. The man in the driver's seat behind

Bill looked Old Guard, a twenty- year man, and probably assumed his nickel partner—Bill had five years in—was his last hurrah. Cops who could call their own shift and partner like that had to have pull with the desk sergeant.

"Bay Village, eh?" I said. "No offense, Bill, but you're Beat Blue, street detail. What's your interest?"

"Personal. Please, look into it and get back to me."

I told him I would, but I had to air the commentary inside my head. "About your partner over there. Twenty years in and he's still walking the beat. Either he does it for love, or he's peed in somebody's garden once too many. Which is it?"

"He's in twenty-seven years."

"Not answering my question, Bill. Fine. What's with Bay Village?"

"Somebody I know is MIA, which is why I'm asking you." Bill handed me his card. I flipped it over for pertinent details. Bill wanted Homicide. He had written out the 5Ws for me. Who, What, When, Where, and Why. The methodology traced back to the ancient Greeks. Bill was off to a good start, but a slot for the detective's exam and for a desk was a matter of a test score and beaucoup politics. No help that the department disliked homosexuals. Yeah, Bill was one of them. I scanned his list.

"Looks good, but I'd add an H next time."

"H?"

"How for method used. How could tell you lots about the killer or victim, or both."

"Good to know," Bill said. "Look, there's a catch with my request." I waited for it. "Talk to Jimmy C. Start with him."

"Suspect?"

"A lead. Information"

"I'll see what I can do. I've got to go."

"I owe you one, Shane."

"Famous last words, after I'll call you in the morning."

That made Bill laugh, and I watched him amble his way to the cruiser. "One last thing, though," I called out. He turned to catch what I had to say.

"Eyes open and your back to the wall, brother." I lifted my chin to remind him of the car behind him. He gave me a mock salute.

Hearing the name Jimmy C made my breakfast repeat itself. I had the picture snapped and developed right there. The question was the frame of reference and Bill's angle. It could be that Bill wanted me to talk to the Renaissance man of crime before anyone in the BPD talked to him, assuming they could find him. Jimmy was a man of many skills. Disappearance was one of his many fortes. I had a name and address for Who and Where of his MISPER on the back of his card. The When and Why had fat question marks after them.

I stood there. Bill pulled his nightstick out of its holster so he could get into the passenger side of the car. Boston Police Department cars resembled taxicabs, often the same make and model, same color scheme, same detail, but there were two major differences: the quality of the ride and the fare.

The car crawled past me, as did the hard stare of the cop behind the wheel. His face, a mix of mean and irritation from a dull razor, declared me lower than a streetwalker, unfit for sunlight. Cops divide the world into Citizens and Assholes. His consideration of me said I ranked beneath both.

The traffic light changed, the car pulled away, and I tried not to cough in the wake of exhaust fumes. I possessed a second calling card in less than twenty-four hours. First, in the livery service to Beacon Hill, and now this. I had to find Jimmy to hear what he had to say about Bill's missing person. Another Jimmy had disappeared in Detroit in July, but everyone knew what had happened to James Riddle Hoffa. The questions there were Who and How, not Why.

I had an epiphany on the other side of Summer Street. Such moments of grace don't visit me often. The idea came to me when I saw the street art, orange lollipops twirling like a dervish in the gusts of wind that ripped through downtown. There was a coffee shop nearby.

Coffee shops are the halfway houses of every city, where each adult can fuel up with the spare change in their pocket. Booze first thing in the morning said a man was unreliable. Tea was un-American, but the counter of a coffee shop is democracy. I had a place in mind.

Eddie's was a recess in a brick wall that swallowed customers one at a time through a narrow door. The astringent scent of coffee preceded it, and the veil of smoke near the door was the gauntlet. Inside, if you could squeeze in sideways past the person leaving, there was a large counter. A Joe or Jane would place an order, get their coffee and shove off.

I saw my man and he saw me. Perhaps the bell above the door tolled off-key when I entered. That revelation I had earlier? Eddie was a CI, a confidential informant. Past tense, used to be, but he owed me large, regardless whether I wore a shield or not.

"Hello, Eddie. Coffee, please, for here."

"Long time, no see," he said, forearms on the counter, after he poured me a cup. The nautical tattoos on his forearms, once proud, were now gray and shrunken. His jutted chin directed me to the far end of the counter. I walked parallel to the destination with my cup. Customers at the end vacated the space, understanding it as Eddie's temporary office for a tête-à-tête.

"I need to place an order," I said to him. His grip on the ubiquitous hand-towel loosened. He understood my request as code. Eddie was the switchboard for criminal talent. He should have been a telephone operator, but I couldn't see him sitting all day in a chair, or on roller-skates. Eddie connected people promptly, politely, for a small fee and did it with efficiency, without asking too many details.

"What do you need?"

I thought of the long list of Jimmy's talents, deciding on one that would appeal to his pride. I needed Jimmy interested enough to meet me.

"I need a light."

"But you don't smoke," Eddie said before he slapped my hand on the counter. "Kidding. I've got just the guy for you. I beckoned Eddie close enough to lean in and whisper Jimmy's name. He nodded. "The very man I had in mind." Eddie's eyes met mine. "Meet cute?"

He knew I enjoyed cinema and understood the term for a meeting between kindred souls, except Jimmy was not anyone's idea of romance. I waited for Eddie to make the call and arrange the meet. Jimmy didn't meet with a client unless vetted. Eddie screened applicants. Do it wrong, and you'll end up in a barrel in Boston Harbor.

Asking for a light meant I wanted a torch, an arsonist. Lightning bug was another password for a skilled artist of the flame. A professional had to know the science of detection, how to dodge the fire chief, and how insurance adjusters snooped after the owner filed a claim. I dawdled over my cup of coffee while I waited.

"Visit the MFA," Eddie said when he returned.

"Museum of Fine Arts?"

Eddie hunched forward. "There's a boutique across from the Indian."

That was about as precise a set of instructions as I was going to get from Jimmy. I didn't expect Jimmy to provide directions in Smoots, the units some engineer at MIT used to measure the Salt and Pepper Shaker Bridge between Boston and Cambridge years ago. I thanked Eddie and left a Washington on the counter. A pittance for an audience with Jimmy.

The little man inside my head was throwing things around the attic to get my attention. He stomped up and down in protest, telling me business with Jimmy amounted to a fare I couldn't pay.

I looked above the counter at the prices on my way out. Cost of business had gone up for coffee shops. The price of sugar shot up, along with the cost of a pound of coffee, on account of a frost in Brazil, but Eddie didn't pinch his customers. He charged a nickel a cup.

Outside, the street reeked of stale cigarettes. The breeze wafted in a taste of the ocean on winter's breath. I did an Army cadence in my head to soothe the dissident between my ears. I had the obstacle course that was public transport, train or bus, ahead of me.

The MFA was on Huntington Avenue. The Indian Eddie mentioned was a statue of a Native American on a horse on the lawn in front of the museum, head cocked back to the heavens since its creation in 1909, either with the resignation of Christ on the cross at what the Pale Faces had done to his people, or waiting for a pop fly from the baseball stadium that used to sit up the street. Eddie said Jimmy's shop was across Huntington Avenue, opposite the museum.

I had never met the man. Jimmy C or Jimmy the C, as he was known by either moniker. His reputation preceded him as dark and mysterious, dangerous but principled. He didn't kill people, though he defended himself. He didn't heist people, though he fenced items. I couldn't separate the yolk from the whites, the fact or fiction about Jimmy, but I had a hot case of nerves.

I was back to rucking, back to the weight of thoughts inside my head as I walked to the bus stop. The man inside my head reached the same conclusion. Few things scared Jimmy and to me that's a dangerous man.

People around me huddled and, without any training, formed a line to board a yellow-skirted Flyer bus that lurched to a stop at the curb. Brakes released air and the doors slapped open. The passengers exiting the transport barked calls for decency, jostled and shoved their way out to the sidewalk. Salmon had it easier swimming to their ancestral grounds. I boarded, paid my fare, and found a seat. I read the road over the top of the newspaper in front of me.

Chapter 4: Sports Night

The shop was where Eddie said it would be. I walked in, a bell tinkled to announce my presence. The tall Jimmy had his hair whiffled to the scalp. In a tailored shirt from one of the high-end shops on Newbury Street, he wore a watch on his left wrist like most people, which meant he was right-handed. No ring, wedding band or otherwise, on either hand. The rest of him hid behind a shop counter. Jimmy's cheekbones were high and tight, giving his face the mask of a deadly harlequin, whether he was happy or sad. He had a voice that would get him a drink after last call. I said hello to Jimmy.

"We've never met, have we?" he asked.

"We have not. Eddie referred me," I said, cold and calm. A guy like Jimmy didn't believe in luck, didn't believe in little talking birds either, so I played honest as an altar boy in the sacristy.

"Eddie," he said and his eyes narrowed. "A job, then?"

Again, I chose purity. "No job. I need information."

"I'm many things, but a rat ain't one of them. I despise rodents, and I don't work with people I don't know."

Jimmy starched the point the way Jimmy Cagney menaced. I had to break the egg.

"You do know me, or I should say, know of me."

"We doing pirouettes, or what? Tell me what is it you want, and maybe I'll orient you in the right direction."

"I'm looking for Roger Sherman," I said and watched the man's eyebrows do an Olympic lift. I continued with details. "He lives in Bay Village, but something tells me you knew that. What you don't know is he's missing and, without naming names, a friend, who isn't a client, is concerned."

I explained to Jimmy who I was and what I did for a living.

"If Roger is missing, then I'm concerned," Jimmy said, face somewhat relaxed. There was some kind of connection between Jimmy and this Roger that went beyond business. A face didn't run that fast through emotions and Jimmy's had done the hundred-yard dash.

"You're a friend of Roger's?" I asked. He nodded, so I put it to him gentle and compassionate. "Not asking you to snitch, Jimmy, but what could you tell me that might help?"

"Saw him two nights ago. Sports night."

"Boys' night out for some beers and a game. Celtics or Bruins?"

"Brewins." He said it like a true Bostonian and waved me forward for some privacy despite the empty boutique. The place was wall-to-wall arts and crafts and sundry knick-knacks that made no business sense. The shop had to be a front and about as real as the Better Business Bureau plaque on the far wall.

"Nice fedora there," I said, distracted. I eyed the hat under the glass counter. Gray felt, medium brim and back bland. More Spade than Marlowe.

"Royal Stetson," Jimmy said. "Want to give it a try? You can carry it off."

"Why do you say that?"

"You remind me one of those detectives from those old black-and-white movies. Minus the trench coat, though. You're not good looking, a little banged up, and you reek of damage, which is why I say you can pull it off."

"Thanks for the boost and knock, Jimmy. You sure know how to make a guy feel white."

"See what I mean?" He pointed a finger at me. "You talk like them. Not sure why you do, but you do, and that's no dig. Besides, the ladies don't care for a man who looks better than them."

"Why is that?" I asked.

"Makes them uneasy and insecure."

The fedora was a temptation, a distinctive look from the lids on men in the streets, and the price on the little tag that sneaked out from under the brim, reasonable. I shelved the idea, thinking the hat amounted to an old man's look, like a pince-nez in a T.S. Eliot poem.

I gave his place the once-over so he'd notice that I was capable of the obvious, and laid out what I was thinking. "Mind me asking, what kind of show are you running here? I didn't expect to find you operating a Bed and Breakfast for Sox fans on the pilgrimage trail to Fenway."

"Back to Roger, please," he said, and I respected his commitment to business.

"Any clue why he would disappear? Did he owe money?"

"Man paid his bills, above and under the table."

"Good to know. Is he on the outs with someone that he'd have to lay low?"

"Not that I know of."

"Just how well do you know him?"

Jimmy straightened up. I didn't like the expression on his face. I saw his hand on the counter curl into a fist. The slow intake of breath said Jimmy was thinking about how he would answer the question.

"Roger is a good guy. He doesn't have any enemies, and he's no chicken. When he has a problem, he confronts it, solves it, and moves on."

"Solve any of those problems with a phone call to you?"

"Roger is a close friend."

"Tell me more about sport's night."

"Roger is the host. I'll leave it at that."

We stared at each other. That answer was a turnstile to a lot of possibilities.

"You'll leave it at that?" I bobbed my head in frustration and rapped the countertop. "Great. A man has disappeared and that's all you've got for me. I thought we were friends, Jimmy."

"It's temporary."

We had reached a stalemate and I was worried that Jimmy would take it upon himself to conduct his own investigation. Which made me worry about Bill.

This was Jimmy C, a man for whom the C was the kindling for speculation. One story said the C alluded to his outsized member and that at one time he starred in blue films. The counter obscured visual confirmation, thankfully. Another story related his love for a bird, a cockatoo, but I didn't see a perch, feathers, or any cracked seeds on the floor. Jimmy was no Detective Baretta with his beloved Fred. I cold-eyed him and he paid me back with the stare of a dead fish.

Jimmy C reached under the counter and I reached for my piece. His left hand flew out like a stop sign at a schoolyard crossing. "Relax!"

I had my hand on the stock of my .38, eyes intent on him. Which brings me to the other explanation for the C: that he carried a meat cleaver. That was a story I could believe. "Show me your hands," I said.

"All right. Take it easy. I've got something for you." He jingled a small key ring that he pulled out from under the counter. He orbited a key around the metal circle until the key came off. "This is a key to Roger's place," he said. "You know where in Bay Village?" I nodded. "Take it, but I want it back when you're done. Today. Understood?"

"And if I don't?" I asked.

His glare would have made an entire school of sharks turn tail and dart for deeper waters. I knew he wasn't a murderer, but there's always a first time. We were alone, the swampy Fens weren't too far away, and he had a cleaver.

"Okay, Jimmy. Level with me. What's with the key?"

"Sports night."

"Sports night, huh." I eased my hand away from my chest, away from my gun, my stampeding heart. "Give me time to get over to Bay Village. It's not exactly around the corner."

He checked his watch. I sighed. He had the meter running. I pocketed the key. Thought for a second about that fedora before I walked to the door. I heard his voice behind me. "So, no job?"

"Sorry, Jimmy. That was just a smokescreen to find you," I answered, with my hand on the doorknob. I felt smug about my pun as the door closed behind me. I tried to imagine Jimmy's disappointment. He was no pyromaniac, in the strict sense. Arson happened to be something he was proficient at. Back when I was a cop, I read one theory as to how he started a fire. The method still makes me cringe. He would tie a kerosene-dipped tampon to a rat's tail and let it run loose through the targeted building. Jimmy had been truthful with me.

He hated rats.

Chapter 5: It's A Wrap

Bay Village was a visit to a bygone era. Sidewalks were cobblestone, streets narrow, and streetlamps, gas. The address for Sherman was at the end of Bay Street, clinging to its contemporaries on one side, the roaring Mass Pike on the other.

The abode was cute as a doghouse, about the size of one, too. The chimney on the top of the A-framed roof promised a fireplace inside. A fence the color of an oxidized penny acted as the rude elbow in the tight space between the house and the neighbors next door.

Nothing said Yankee understatement more than red bricks for a façade, mortar faded to chalked lines, and shutters the color of tar. Red and black, Stendhal would've appreciated the color scheme. A front door, painted fire engine red, awaited me behind a black lattice gate. I had four black steps and railing on both sides for the climb up. Had I not had a key to the place, I would've expected a man in a powdered wig in breeches and stockings to answer the door and offer me sherry inside.

I plucked my handkerchief from my back pocket to prevent fingerprints. I stepped onto hardwood floors, tawny from age. The wall panels in each room on the first floor were painted in the bright, boisterous colors of yellow and blue, glossed up with copal varnish. I concluded my admiration with hand-detailed paper borders around the windows. I continued the tour.

There was fresh ash in the fireplace. A trophy-like urn hosted a poker. I moved around chair backs shaped like shields. The updated kitchen included a modern stove and dishwasher. A brazen light signaled that the dishwasher had completed the cycle.

Handkerchief over my hand, I unhinged the stove to find a large sterilizing tray. Inside and on the trays, I found sex toys. The shapes were normal, to those who enjoyed childbirth in reverse. I haven't blushed like that since Ms. Andrews, my elementary school teacher, had unintentionally given me a view of her cleavage while reviewing my spelling with me.

I didn't use the handrail to the second floor. Near the landing, something truly evil crawled up my nose. This was not *Eau de Mort*. I knew that scent. The Reaper's cologne is indescribable, one that I've encountered more times than I cared to remember, from the Army buddy I'd found dead, the maggots devouring skin, to villagers in the fields where they'd been shot. This malodorous presence emanated from one of two rooms on the upper floor. Handkerchief over mouth and nose, my own hot breath against my hand, I proceeded.

Room 1 had for its main attraction a hammock suspended from the ceiling. The stirrups and the bivalve mirrors were not what George Washington would've used for an evening's sleep. Saran Wrap covered the floor. Hockey paraphernalia decorated the room. Helmets and facemasks outnumbered pennants, pucks, jerseys, and hockey sticks.

There was no body, or sign of one.

Room 2 would have delighted Torquemada. More black-and-gold sportswear à la Bruins littered the room. A team manager would've referenced pages on his clipboard to inventory the contents. I saw row after row of devices that I had no idea their intent or application. Again, the plastic flooring, that persistent odor. A mask mounted to the wall intrigued me, so I examined it. My finger sensed a latch and the face swung open. Inside, I found a camera, a small gadget that James Bond would've appreciated. I unhinged the backing to find a roll of film. As I put it inside my coat pocket, I heard stairs creak.

I back-pedaled soft as a ballerina to the door. Footsteps. Someone was downstairs. I pressed my back against the wall, ears alert. The stench thickened in my nose and I wanted to retch. I eased my sidearm out and held it as if I were praying with it.

I waited.

I waited some more, tempted now to crane my head around the doorframe. The footsteps approached. I moved my foot. I swung myself out into the hallway and yelled "Freeze!"

A blow to my wrist from a nightstick sent my weapon flying. Somehow, I saw through the pain. Hurt like hell, I accepted the sting the way Nolan Ryan might catch a pitch without a glove.

"Cleary, you son of a bitch," the voice said.

He pinned my spine to the wall. I smelled sour rye on his breath and counted nose hairs. A witch could cast a spell under the crescent scar on his cheek. We wrestled with that nightstick jammed against my throat. I got to thinking the policeman's baton was the descendant of the medieval mace and this bastard wanted to knight me with it. He kneed me, missing the jewels a fraction of an inch, and I doubled over. He rapped my back hard and down I went. I could count the loops he used in tying his shoelaces.

I grabbed both calves and jammed myself upright, lifting him up, like a lineman after the center snapped the ball. I trucked him across the hallway toward the hammock. Somewhere in transit he torqued my center of gravity. We crashed short of the pleasure sling. The slight rattle of chains teased me. I thought I had him.

"Breaking and entering, are we?" he said.

"Not when I have the key," I yelled back through the rain of blows. I moved my head and missed his fist as it hit the floor. He screamed. Saran Wrap came up with his hand. On me now with his full weight, I was as good as a cord of wood and he was the ax. Bent over me, he pummeled me until I tasted my own blood. I blocked what I could, protected my face with my forearms. Then the rain of blows stopped. I looked up. I lowered my arms.

A meat cleaver was pressed against his throat.

"You move and it's kosher time. Understood?"

The cop nodded. Jimmy the C had a handful of hair in his manicured fingers. The cop peeled himself off me. Jimmy moved him to standing and then to the wall, the cleaver's sharp edge pressed against the man's throat.

I coughed and reacquainted myself with air.

"Take his gun and empty out the bullets," Jimmy instructed me. He pressed the cleaver just enough for the man to squeal and breathe shallow. "While you're at it, check for a drop-piece on him."

"Negative," I reported and shook the rounds into the palm of my hand.

"Good. Let's return the good officer's sidearm to his holster now, where it will be clipped and stay clipped, isn't that right, Officer?" The man grunted agreement. "Excellent," Jimmy said. "You will walk out of this house to your car and drive away. You're here without a partner, but you won't call for backup, or do anything else stupid. You walk away. Nobody needs to know you were here. We in agreement?"

The cop nodded. Jimmy's smile frightened me. This was yeoman's work for him and he liked it, like Mikey from the commercials enjoyed Life cereal. Jimmy released the man, and we watched the cop screw out of the room. We heard the door close seconds later.

"Hope he didn't leave fingerprints," I joked.

"There's more than fingerprints in this place," Jimmy said. He was right. The luminol that the forensic guys used would've lit this room up into an enchanted village for the debauched. I watched Jimmy slide his cleaver into a leather sheath, which he tucked somewhere behind him under his overcoat. "Need a lift?" he asked.

"What I need are answers. Like, why did that guy have a key to this place?" Jimmy held out his hand. I dug into my pocket and gave him his key back.

"Why did you come?" I asked him.

"You're welcome."

"Thanks. Really and truly," I said. "Now tell me why you're here."

"I forgot to tell you something that might help your investigation."

"I wouldn't call it an investigation, Jimmy, but what is it?"

"Roger said he was meeting with a Marty Savitz. Know the name?"

"The sports agent?"

"One and the same."

Jimmy didn't elaborate. We stood there. "So, this is sports night?" I said.

"This is sports night and that copper knew it."

I reviewed the room once more. I glanced up at the ceiling. A lot of care had gone into setting up that hammock. "This place has me thinking, Jimmy.

Quid pro quo?"

"Air out your thoughts and I'll listen."

"You gave me a key and your friend Roger had a key, and so did the cop. Everybody has a key, so that makes me wonder about this gentlemen's club here. Looks to me that you or Roger, or the both of you, are running a service that, for a premium, members have a private playpen where they can act out their fantasies, but there is one problem. Scheduling."

Jimmy didn't blink an eye, or move a muscle, to indicate whether I was hitting the nail wrong. The Saran Wrap crinkled and stuck to the soles of my shoes like fresh bubblegum.

"Place is secluded," I said to advance my theory. "Streets around here are tight. Which means clientele have privacy, and nobody would know they're here because there are no cars parked anywhere. Nice setup, especially if you're a VIP."

Near the window, I pulled aside a shade, glanced down at the street.

"A well-placed spotter would know who was coming and going. Sports night is theme night, and there are other themes. How am I doing?"

"Good so far," Jimmy said.

"Whether you're running this or Roger is doesn't matter to me," I said upwind to the tall man. "Discretion is paramount; violate that and your reputation is down the tubes, out to the Harbor with the sewer. That's motive in my book. People kill to protect their money and their secrets. What do you think?"

"You think Roger is dead?"

"It's possible."

"I'm a little more optimistic than you, Shane. I'd like to keep it to Roger being missing. You've already toe-tagged him and there isn't even a body."

"Odds aren't in Roger's favor. Give me names."

"I can't," Jimmy said.

"Privileged?"

"It's simpler than that: I don't know." Jimmy twirled his finger in the air. "This was Roger's thing. He ran it and he was a clam about who came and went, when and how and with whom. Perhaps your friend, who put you up to this, knows more than he's letting on."

I hadn't seen that one coming. I holstered my lost firearm after I wiped it down from its nap on the floor.

"Find Roger, and do it before the cops do," Jimmy said and pushed past me, impatient and somewhat preoccupied. I watched him cross the room. I waited until he got to the door.

"Jimmy?"

He turned and waited for my question. He didn't move, didn't convey any emotion. "What does the C stand for?" I asked.

"What is it to you?"

"You know, Jimmy, I'd get an answer from fresh sheetrock before I'd get one from you." My answer made his lip twitch.

"Constantino," he said. He furthered the explanation, with a hint of pride. "People have heard of Jimmy the Weasel, or Jimmy the Greek, so I took the C for my handle. Anything else?"

"One last question." I sniffed hard. "What is that smell?"

"Crisco."

"Shortening?" I said, confused.

He evaluated the room, eyes spending the most time on the Saran Wrap. "It's not just for cooking. Sure you don't want a ride?"

"Yes, I'm sure."

Chapter 6: Hot Whisper

I wearied myself up the stairs to my office inside the Jewelers Building on Washington Street, my home away from my home in the South End. That's the South End as in south of Back Bay, not to be confused with South Boston, where desegregation lit a fuse that had been smoldering since Reconstruction. I glanced over the railing down to the lobby. The marble floor sparkled.

Built when Prohibition raged, the Jewelers Building was where a Boston Brahmin, a businessman from the Financial District, a jazzman, or King Solomon, a gangster from my neighborhood, could walk in and shop, side by side, for diamonds, pearls, and sapphires under secured glass counters.

The personnel to any of the one hundred offices in the building would choke the elevator during business hours. All that staff, all those people necessary for precious gems was not what I imagined the patriots against a tax on tea leaves had in mind when they organized against King George at the Old South Meeting House, two minutes away from me on Washington Street.

Clean and cold as a mausoleum, the building was silent as the grave at this morning hour, unlike my apartment building. There, I could pass several dark wood doors and hear the sounds of a game show and an argument with the television at any hour of the day or night.

Television had never appealed to me. I'd rather sit in front of a typewriter instead of an idiot box. Many a good man and woman have typed out the lines of their lives, carriage return after carriage return, day after day, month after month, and year after year until the bell dinged, if they heard it at all,

37

and most of them screamed when they did.

The third floor to my apartment in Union Park was not entirely mine. I shared it with an ancient tailor and a mysterious financier of imports and exports. The three of us were like actors in a silent film, with fast appearances, faster disappearances, and mouths that moved to the subtitles of hi and bye.

Until I settled the overdue rent, I would have to miss the place, sounds and sights alike. My apartment overlooked a club of trees outside, a healthy island of grass in the middle, and two smooth blacktops for parked cars. I had two rooms, a kitchenette, and a bathroom that I could sneeze through during hay fever season.

Here in the Jewelers Building, I had an office Spade or Marlowe could respect, a kitchen big enough for a coffee pot, a hot plate, and a mouse for a guest. Delilah made certain that last item never happened. My luxury of luxuries was that I had a private water closet, a WC, as it was called in the Twenties. My commode could pass as a twin for the one Michael Corleone visited in *The Godfather*. Like the one in the movie, I learned that the overhead tank was an excellent hiding spot.

If I wanted more than a bird's bath in my bathroom sink, I'd visit the gym on the corner of Tremont Street and Temple Place, where 'Evenings for young men' and 'physical culture' included fisticuffs and lonely bouts of solitaire. The manager there ran a clean establishment. The towels were fresh, the showers looked after. There was no recurrence of riff-raff, theft, or one incident of toe fungus.

I shopped for my keys, surprised not to hear a mew or scratch on the other side of the wood. I turned the lock and eased the door open, expecting Delilah at my feet.

My nose twitched. L'odeur dangereux. I knew that scent. It wasn't brimstone, but it might as well have been cordite with a spritz of sulfur.

I opened the door and there she was, a naughty angel perched on my desk. She was angled back, the weight on the palms of her hands behind her. I bet she had etched in grips for traction.

"Cat," I said. "You shouldn't be here."

I was on the receiving end of her eyes doing the slow appraisal. Delilah sat in the doorway to the bathroom. The beating I had received at Sherman's place dropped fast from memory. Not one mew from Delilah. Her dark eyes acknowledged me for one hot second, then looked at the intruder on our desk. When Delilah's head turned back to me, she blinked contempt.

"You look terrible," Cat said. "What happened? Do you need some ice?"

"I'm fine. Occupational hazard, and I don't have any ice. Lost the recipe."

"Aren't we in a mood?" she said

I unbuttoned my coat as I took her in. One long pillar of a leg draped down. No shoes, no socks or stockings. No nothing. I could count every hand-painted toe. I saw folded clothes on the leather. The sofa was mine; the clothes were hers. I tried to act angry, outraged when I asked, "How did you get in?"

"Through the keyhole. I read that somewhere."

"Sounds like a line from a movie," I said.

Her chin lifted, she said, "Can't you do something about the cat? Feeling judged."

"Excuse me," I said and used my foot to shoo Delilah into the bathroom and shut the door. It was something a slug would do, and the sound of the latch compounded how slimy I felt doing that to Delilah.

I racked the coat and took off my suit jacket next with a slow yawn. I hurt. Cat held one knee and watched. I ached. She was the centerpiece of a triptych formed by two windows behind her. Blinds pulled down, she left enough of the window open so the world outside could breathe for us. I undid the shoulder holster next.

"Nice pea shooter there," she said. "Thirty-eight, right?"

"Smith and Wesson. Three-inch barrel."

"Why don't you carry an automatic?"

"Because they jam and you don't want a useless piece of steel once it's out." I hung the holster on a peg and undid the buttons on my cuffs next.

"Are you going to come over here? I don't bite," she said.

"Biting isn't what I'm worried about. May I ask what you told your husband? He must know you're not home."

"I wish you wouldn't say it like that." She puffed a wisp of hair away. A feint of mild annoyance she had perfected in her teen years.

"I'll rephrase," I said like a lawyer. "Does he know you're here?" A petulant look was my answer. I redirected with, "Does your driver, the one who resembles Dick Butkus, know you're in this room?"

"That big lug?"

"Yeah, him. Butkus is known for biting people when he's frustrated," I said.

"You sound scared of him."

"Not scared of your driver," I said. "I have enough sense not to expose my ankles, or anything else around the man. Let's have it, Cat. What line did you feed him?"

"Told him I wanted to go shopping. I ditched him at Filene's. I said a girl needs her space, and he could take a long lunch."

"And he bought it?"

"He does what he's told."

She'd laced her answer with enough cyanide, I smelled almonds.

I dished it right back at her. "'Does what he's told.' Same thing could be said of dogs. I suppose your man behind the wheel is loyal and on a leash."

"Now you sound jealous." Her lips tightened as if she'd tasted something sour. "I suppose you can say he's loyal; it's an admirable quality in a person. He was the one servant my parents had, and he came with me when I married. Are we done with cross-examination? There's another reason I'm here."

I stood in front of her now. I considered her lips. Her eyes, brown with specks of gold, met mine. Her hands grasped my sides but I held back just enough to feel her nails scrape my ribs.

"Oh, and that reason is?" I asked.

"Bray will call you later." The fingernails had a different effect when I heard his name. "There's been a development. He received a demand. Fifty thousand dollars."

"You didn't come all this way to tell me that."

"I thought it important and I wanted to tell you myself. Can't you see I dressed for the occasion?"

"I can see that," I said and tried not to look, but did.

"What do you think Bray should do?" she asked.

"He should pay it and be done with it. His real-estate deal is worth a whole lot more."

A foot rubbed against the inside of my right thigh.

"Fifty thousand per copied page, Shane. Do you have any idea how much that...I'd wish to hell you wore a tie. You know I want some sugar."

She lunged forward, her hands on my shirt, pulling at it and yanking the tails up. Her hair stuck to the side of my face. My brain calculated the math, price per page times the number of copied pages in my possession, when I felt her, warm against me and under me.

It started with a kiss and hands. Later, much later, her warm breath was in my ear, and her words played there, and we ended and began again, her and me, with her hot whisper in my ear.

Chapter 7: Smell A Rat

That was that. Our goodbyes were chaste, awkward. She left and I stayed in my office chair. I didn't move for some time before I opened the bathroom door to let Delilah out. She wouldn't look at me and I didn't blame her. I doled out some food as a meagre penance. Delilah ignored the dish.

My Catholic upbringing kicked in. I thought about adultery when I returned to my desk. Everything in the room conspired to remind me of sin. A cold breeze blew in. I'd forgotten that she had lifted the window up. I pressed down on the sash and met resistance. I put some shoulder into it, to close the damn thing. The window refused. When it closed at last, the frame creaked and the pane shuddered. I threw myself into my chair, only to learn that the wood was unforgiving, too.

I wanted something and I had nothing. I craved a cigarette, but I had quit them. I thought about a drink, a shot of whiskey. No luck. I had a glass but no bottle of anything in any of the drawers. I wanted to talk it out with Delilah but she was in a mood. She padded into the room and disappeared around the back of the sofa we used for a bed.

Satisfaction. I wanted to savor it. There should've been some. I gave Cat what Bray couldn't. I knew it. She knew it. Like old times, the sex was better because I had learned my lessons well. Us together was the stuff people wanted from magazines and movies because we understood each other. We anticipated the when, where, and how, and we could play it clean or dirty without it ever becoming cheap and tawdry.

It was lovely, really, as smooth and hot as the best whiskey on a cold night.

Now it seemed more like a whiskey sour. Cat came. Cat left. I was empty, used up. She'd find her driver and return to Bray. She'd live the pretty life up on the Hill, her every day comfortable and secure, while the rest of us, me included, made do with the hardness that life dished out.

Hardwood floors. Hardback chairs. Concrete mattress. Resentful pet.

Absent the cigarettes, absent the drink, I did what every guy did to work the splinters out. I threw myself into my job. I strapped on protection. I collected my coat and gloves and I evicted myself.

***

I walked it to the Little Building. I turned right outside the front door and headed down Washington Street, toward Filene's and its famous Basement at Downtown Crossing on a typical Boston afternoon. Bitter cold, the streets were wet with puddles. Most of the last snowfall had melted, lost its initial beauty. Driven and salted, the snow had turned gray and black as soot.

I saw the crowd before I experienced them. The Christmas Crush formed in front of me, the wall of flesh trying to squeeze itself through the doors of Filene's. The Basement downstairs was worse. There the rich and poor, the cultured and barbaric shopped in search of steep discounts on expensive brand name items. The sport called shopping was in full rage there, near the subway stop. Few men were present. Women ceased to be women when one of them nosed a bargain in the air. They massed and pushed, a gaggle of broads with deadly intent.

Kids dreaded the downtown stores in two words: school clothes. St. Wystan's spared me that torture. I've legged through all the stores, at one time or another, with my parents as a kid. Gilchrist's, R. H. Stearns, and Jordan Marsh. I visited them all. There was a time, though, when I cocked my head back, wide-eyed and amazed at the Christmas decorations and window displays at these stores. Every year Filene's and Jordan Marsh competed to have the best display window. Every year, caravans of onlookers bunched up on the sidewalk and gaped, pointing at the window and Santa's belly, his sack of toys. They marveled at the clever artistry of fake snow, false winds, and pretend snowbanks. We were innocent. Our parents played along with the charade, before they took us for ice cream and we'd take pictures with

Santa. We didn't think anything of sitting in a strange man's lap. We didn't imagine Kris Kringle as a robber baron who ran a sweatshop in the coldest place on the planet.

I stopped for a moment. Like Cat, it was all nostalgia, a con. The decorations were there, in the same color scheme of red, white, and green. They played at your memories, like Hallmark danced with your emotions. I snapped out of it.

In front of Jordan's, someone from the Salvation Army clanged a bell and demanded wayward change for his kettle. The metallic sound of his bell, the repetitive bark of a carny in a uniform drove me to turn right up Winter Street. Tempted as I was to buy a hot pretzel slathered in mustard from a vendor, a cop on a horse blocked me. The horse didn't intend to frustrate my appetite, but I thought it better business to avoid mounted cavalry. The officer in the saddle loomed fifteen hands above the cobblestones, and he had two-thousand pounds of equine flesh under him, and a baton in his hand that could crack my head like a walnut.

I continued up the hill of Winter Street towards Tremont. I looked left, down the narrow alley to Locke-Ober, the fourth oldest restaurant in the United States, and where dad and me had spent an afternoon, a celebratory late lunch. My first shave, and dad insisted we visit the famous wood-paneled restaurant after he bought me a silk tie at Filene's. "You're a man now," he said. I balked at first because the place was expensive. Dad said we had to have the talk. I blushed, thinking he would talk about the birds and the bees over steak and chops with scalloped potatoes, or a Maine lobster or God forbid, Wiener schnitzel. He read my mind, tousled my hair and said, "Somehow, I think that girl, Cat, beat me to that talk. We need to talk about your future."

And we did. Surrounded by Honduran mahogany, the chairs upholstered with red leather, and the lights dim and atmospheric like one of my film noirs, we discussed careers over juicy steaks. Dad was a foreman for a construction company. A proud union man. He told me in the gentlest way that he loved his work, the men he worked with, but he didn't want that life for me. I deserved better, he said. I shouldn't have to wash my hands after a day's work, or work in the elements, which meant more than the weather. Union beefs. Corruption. I sat and listened with rapt attention, because I loved my father. Respected him. He suggested law, he suggested Harvard but smiled and retracted it. He advocated for Boston College because of Mother Church and the rigorous Jesuits.

I didn't care that the restaurant barred women, although Dad told me the story about the day the burlesque queen, Ann Corio, crashed the restaurant in order to confront a city bigwig about the demolition of the Howard in Scollay Square. She worked there, and Dad regaled me with stories about Gypsy Rose and Sophie Tucker and 'Tillie the Tassel' before he shipped off for the war. He got sad for a moment, not about the past, but because the war bothered him. Dad could turn a smile like a car took the corner, and we were back to our conversation about potential schools and career prospects. Anything that wouldn't require breaking your back or ruining your health. Law. Medicine but not dentistry because, he said, it had to be depressing to look inside people's mouths. He said dentists committed suicide more than any other profession. I don't know if that is true, but it stuck and I never forgot it.

The streets, the Christmas décor, did remind me of my parents. I admit it.

I tried not to think about them. It all started the week before Thanksgiving in '63, the week before the turkey was about to come out of the oven, before the choice of either apple or pumpkin pie for dessert, before JFK's cortege and that sad procession behind the horse, the boots in the stirrups, the First Lady in black and a little boy's salute on the television screen. I can still hear it.

Clop. Clop. Clop. The sounds of that dark horse.

My father had survived so much: Guadalcanal in World War II, the fifteen days of Naktong in Korea. I didn't understand the man then. I do now.

In the fifty-two days between Jack Kennedy and '64, my father would kill himself while my mother was out doing errands, and my mother would drop dead of a heart attack from a broken heart. Fifty-two days.

The *Iliad* is fifty-two days long, Lindsey reminded me of that once. Fifty-two days marked the duration of the feud between Agamemnon and Menelaus, the friendship between Achilles and Patroclus, the rage of Achilles against Hector. I had my own anger. Achilles had taken his wrath into the field. I retreated into movies at the National Theatre. I became Marlowe, the tough knight in this damaged world of ours. I would pull down my hat as a visor and turn up my coat collar. I had to. In the short span of those fifty-two days, I had lost my parents, what little innocence was left, and my home. My war had just begun.

I checked my pants pocket for change. I found a dime from Lindsey. I had Braddock's business card, the one I had found on the cushion next to me that night. I was curious about the phone number on the back.

I spotted an alcove where some office stragglers on break slurped coffee and puffed cigarettes. A payphone. I deposited the dime and dialed. A woman's voice answered. I didn't say a word at first because I was stunned.

"Cat?"

"Shane, is that you? How did you get this number?"

"Wouldn't you like to know?"

"I would, actually," she said, and not all that pleasantly either.

"Hubby's business card, on the seat the night I was chauffeured."

"Where are you?"

"On the job. I work for your husband, remember?"

"Not in your office then?"

"No," I said. "I'm out and about."

"I must be losing my touch. Thought you'd need time to recover after that rather athletic performance."

"I take vitamins. Look, I gotta go. Bye," I said.

I hung up the payphone. I dipped my finger into the coin return. Nada. Always thought the odds were better with Ma Bell than with the lottery. I practiced some Evelyn Wood Speed Reading on all the graffiti on the steel around the phone. There was a very popular girl in Chelsea named Chelsea. She wasn't teaching algebra.

There on Tremont, I could see the Little Building ahead, the Boston Common across the street. Everywhere, was history. The Common is the oldest park in the nation, a cow pasture turned into an Olmstead gem, once the parade ground for troops in Colonial days and a scenic place for public hangings, too, as well as the site for the first organized football game in the nation. I contemplated the gold dome of the State House in the distance. The wooden dome had been first covered with copper, then painted gray, and then yellow, and finally gilded in gold leaf until the Second World War required it be blackened for the Nazi planes that never arrived. Everything in this town with any glitter is a con job.

Brayton singled out an accountant named Dunbar. The telltale thumbprint on the photostats led me to the Little Building, thanks to Lindsey's keen eyes and memory. I had to make a go of this lead.

The Little is Modern Gothic and its designer, Clarence Blackall, was responsible for just about every theatre building in the city. Name a venue for drama and he designed it. His delinquent child, The Pilgrim, was one block over. A large pink neon sign crowed a run of movies for the demimonde there. Last time my eyesight wandered down Washington Street *Story of Joanna* was part of a triple-X feature. The Pilgrim's legacy will be that *Deep Throat* played there and the cast received federal indictments for conspiracy to distribute obscenity. From Winthrop's sermon of 'City on the Hill' on the ship *Arbella* to State House dome to sleaze within three city blocks is Boston for you.

***

A black security guard sat at the reception desk. He was a thin man in a blue shirt with a dark tie splashed down his chest. The tie bar looked like an unfinished bridge over shallow water. "May I help you?"

"I'm here to meet someone. Third floor," I said and pointed to the elevators.

"Who is it that you wish to see?"

"Pardon me?"

"I said who is that you wanted to see?"

He had the phone pulled to his ear, ready for a name from me. The piglet curls of the cord stretched tight. The corners of his mouth dropped, his moustache formed a dark circumflex with some gray in it, while he waited for an answer. Good skin and prominent cheekbones made it impossible for me to guess his age. I played dumb and lost to avoid suspicion.

I fumbled for the business card inside my trousers. I shielded the front of it, and squinted, reading the back of it as if I had forgotten my spectacles. "Last name is Dunbar."

"Who shall I say is calling?"

"Fletcher. John Fletcher"

I chose the name of a contemporary of Shakespeare's for an alias since Marlowe was already taken. I shoved both hands deep into my pockets, something I did whenever lied. I waited until the receiver did a slow descent to the cradle.

"I'm afraid there's no Mr. Dunbar on the third floor." Our eyes met, and then, as if by some miracle, his expression changed altogether, like that of someone caught on *Candid Camera*. His voice came out warmer than Santa after one too many rounds of cheap beer at the VFW Hall. He waved a bony finger. "I know you from somewhere."

"I doubt it."

He shook his head. "I never forget a face. It'll come to me. Just a sec." I didn't need this. His fingers drummed the desktop. "You're that cop from the Douglas case."

"I think you're mistaken."

The last thing I wanted was attention. I glanced over my shoulder and saw a patrolman on his beat and that made me itchy. Cops often come into office buildings and chatted with security, as a way to size up the clientele for favors and business on the side. It didn't matter that I'd done nothing wrong. Sin was real, penance was real, but absolution was neither. The boys didn't need an excuse to pulp me with their blackjacks and that was the appetizer before the grinder at the station house. The real fun happened there, in a dark room down the hall, and under city streets.

Another light slap on the wood jarred me.

"Fletcher, my ass. You're that guy." He wagged his finger again. "Shane something or other, with an Irish last name." He shook his head. "Told you I never forget a face."

Maybe we'd crossed paths once, as in I'd squeezed one of his friends for information. He mentioned the Douglas case. Perhaps he possessed an cidetic memory of days past when I prowled the D-Street Housing Project

48

for any intelligence on Officer Douglas. The beat was tense after a sniper picked off seventeen-year-old Charles Pratt. South Boston turned ugly in '73 and justice moved slower than it took for Pratt to bleed out against a wall. I had worked the Pratt neighborhood. Same building, same project, and then came along Douglas who shot a kid and hid behind the badge.

I had my right foot poised for an about-face the Army had drilled into me. I showed my palms and smiled. "I should go. I think I got the wrong building."

"Relax, man, and come over here." He encouraged me to step to the side, which took me out of view of the main entrance and any police on Boylston Street. The guard's voice continued its casual tone. "I saw you at a party once."

"A party?"

I heard a low bass for a laugh, unexpected in such a thin man. Our eyes met again. This time I knew we were friends.

"That party, my friend, was for the man you helped exonerate, and my girl is his second cousin. That's how I remember your face."

"You don't say. Sorry, I don't recall yours."

"And you white folks say we all look alike." He enjoyed a rumbling, snickering laugh. When he stopped, he asked, "What is it you need, brother?"

"Dunbar. I was told he worked here."

"Second floor. There are four pavilions there, but I can't tell you which one he's in. The cat is Manhattan Project classified or something. Name isn't even in the directory. He takes the elevator to the second floor and—"

"I was told third floor."

The man shook his head. "I think I know what happened. This building has a mezzanine between the ground floor and the first floor. Easy enough to confuse and some folks count the mezzanine as a floor."

"What can you tell me about the man?"

"Not much. Only saw him once or twice. Little man, about five-foot four, a Poindexter, dresses sharp, and he carries a weird briefcase."

"Weird how?" I asked.

"Little padlocks on it. I wouldn't be surprised if he handcuffed himself to it."

"Hours?"

"Nothing to set your watch to, if that's what you mean. Some days he's in and out early, and other days he stays late. I know because I rotate through two shifts."

"Talk to him?" I asked.

"Nah, man. I stay on the down low. I do my rounds and fill out this here sandbox." He showed me the clipboard with a box of squares. "I so much as smile at any of the secretaries here and I'm out of a job. They're white, and I'm black. Separation of powers, just like the United States Constitution promised, know what I'm saying?" I nodded and listened to this fount of free information flow. "There're hundreds of offices in this place, restaurants and shops, and underground access to the subway. This joint is a city unto itself. Hell, there's even a Post Office in this building."

"A Post Office?" I said. Another surprise.

He held out a closed fist. He turned that hand over and uncurled his long fingers. He had a present for me in the palm of his hand. Keys. "This little piggy opens a door." His eyes indicated where. "This little piggy here opens the only office door on the mezzanine. You can't miss it. Stairs are over there." He tapped that smallish key twice.

"Private, huh?"

"Exclusive," he said and pulled the sleeve over his wristwatch and said, "Smokers' Lounge. I'd say in about five minutes your man will take his cigarette break."

"How do I avoid suspicion since I'm not part of the Manhattan Project?"

"Allow me," he said and pulled at my suit jacket lapel. He dabbed a simple adhesive white dot there. "Them lawyer-types use these all the time," he said. "Sometimes they change up the colors, too."

"Thanks." I peeled off my winter coat. My jacket puckered and he saw that I was carrying. He took the overcoat and stowed it beneath his counter. Nobody was around and I didn't see any cameras in the usual places. Mr. Security seemed to have more advice for me.

"If he asks, tell him you're with the firm." He turned sideways to show me the company's name on the flash on his shoulder. "We've got specialist

50

managers who don't wear uniforms and, yeah, some do carry heat, so you'll look the part."

"What if he asks me specifics about the building?" I asked.

"Paranoid any?"

"Prepared is more like it."

He gave some facts known only to insiders. Good thing the Army taught me the memory game they had lifted from Kipling called KIM. It came in handy, like now. An orphan in India was shown stones and gems, which were then covered over, and he had to say how many stones he had seen and name the type of gems on the tray. KIM. Keep in Mind.

"I'll watch your jacket," he told me, and handed me a business card with hours and days of the week he worked on the back of it.

***

The key to the lounge opened a door to a longish corridor. I walked in with authority and confidence, until I realized I had no cigarettes on me. The room itself was eccentric. Not quite the social center you'd expect for a smoker's lounge. Not a single newspaper lying around. The ashtrays were cheap and wafer-thin, shaped like Chinese throwing-stars. A Panton Chair sat in one corner, and nearest to me were two office chairs, bright orange, a decade out of fashion and faded to the color of a melted creamsicle. I heard someone at the door behind me.

Dunbar walked into an ambush. The pinstriped Bonwit Teller suit said he wasn't hurting enough that blackmail would ease any financial woes. He appeared about fifty. Silver cufflinks. No wedding ring. The onyx pinky ring men wore always baffled me. He wore a soft blue shirt with spread collar, solid tie, probably silk, in a Windsor knot, and a vest. He rehabilitated my notion of what an accountant should look like. He mindlessly searched for a cigarette from the soft pack in his hand. I recognized the brand; it wasn't one of those popular low-tar brands. He snapped his light shut when he saw me.

"Jesus, you scared the daylights out of me," he said.

"Sorry about that. I was checking out the room." I imitated an officer, and placed my hands behind my back and looked around. I rapped my knuckles against the wall here and there, grimaced once in a while, contemplated the ceiling and shook my head.

"Is there any problem?"

"Several," I said. "Lighting is poor. The décor...I wouldn't know where to begin. Moreover, for a smoker's lounge there isn't a fire extinguisher anywhere in sight. The number of sprinklers seems inadequate, which tells me the layout was a custom job, and a poorly designed one at that."

"I see your point," he said, revisiting the same territory my eyes searched before he asked, "Work for an insurance company?"

"Do *you*? Just kidding." The man's face was as placid as an undisturbed bed sheet.

"People don't come in here and stay long," he said. "They smoke their cig and leave."

I approached close enough to impose on him. Dominate him a little. I had height on him and I was betting with the house's money that this guy had a Napoleon complex, along with the sartorial overcompensation.

"In my experience," I said, "a room like this is used for two things, both of them recreational." I gave him a conspiratorial smile to see if one would light up his face, but none did. "Smoke a cigarette, or smoke a little grass, or—"

"In case you haven't noticed there isn't that cannabis smell," he said with an exhalation of whitish smoke. I tried not to choke. Rule that one out: nobody uses the word cannabis.

"Name is Dunbar, right?"

"You're not an indemnity man. My guess is security?"

"Consultant with Furey Security, if you must know."

"I don't recall seeing any fees for a consultation," he said.

"Why should you?" I said, and added, "where's the fun if it isn't secret?"

He was almost done with his cigarette. He would either toast another one, just to keep our exchange going, or he would march right off the playing field to his big desk and pick up the phone and rattle the food chain about some consultant on the premises. He offered me a cigarette after he mashed his dead one into one of the ashtrays. I declined.

"Security, you said. Have to know the lay of the land in your kind of work."

"Indeed." And just like a scene of good guy meets the villain, our roles had been reversed. I was answering his questions now. He put a cigarette to his lip and let it hang there like Bogart, unlit. "How many offices are in this building?" he asked.

"Six hundred."

"Stores?"

"All depends on how you define store."

"Restaurants?"

"Trick question. There's an Automat in the basement."

The cigarette lifted with the smile. "I'm impressed. You knew my last name, but not my first. Anything else you know about me?"

"Tut-tut, Mr. Dunbar, it's no fun to reveal all, but I'll say this," I whispered, "You aren't in any directory, or connected to any one of those six hundred offices."

That made him grin. "I'm something of a consultant myself. I look out for my client's interest, like you do." He checked his watch. "Seems I've exceeded the time I allotted for my break. Good day." We shook hands. He walked a few feet, stopped and turned around.

"Is there something wrong?" I asked.

"Not at all. By the way, it's Danny Dunbar."

"Robert Fletcher."

I watched him leave, cigarette glued to his lower lip. He had decided at the last second to reveal his first name and he counted on the same courtesy from me. He knew I was lying, though. I knew that he was, too, by the way he said Danny. For a man that natty to not use the proper-sounding Daniel was like Queen Victoria calling herself Vicky.

I smelled a rat.

Chapter 8: The Sweet Science

In the trudge back to the office I saw Ma Bell again, this time on the corner of Washington and Kneeland, near New England Medical Center. I've always thought it bad luck to make a call from a payphone in front of a hospital, or in front of a police station, but that didn't stop me from seeing whether another dime might garner me a new deal. I needed a leash on this Dunbar character before he found out I wasn't Fletcher. He would, but the question was how soon.

I skirted the Zone, looked north of Washington Street. The patrol car was a Chevy Nova with plates I recognized. A cop directed traffic there on the corner of Washington and Essex. Bill's senior partner. I watched pedestrians on the street and others exit the Chinatown subway stop in front of his outstretched arms. I dialed the number for the pizza joint nearby where Bill did his sit-and-chew.

"Prince of Pizza, may I help you?" a man answered. I pictured a squat Greek answering the line, hands white from flour and an apron tight around his distended belly. I've enjoyed his pies numerous times. Good food, honest guy.

"The cop near the window," I said. "Tell him Jerome wants a word."

"Yeah, sure. Hold on."

I heard him call Bill. Jerome was code between us. The Jerome Brothers ran the Intermission Lounge a block down the street, among other venues in the Combat Zone. The Venus Brothers had sewn up the rest of the bag in the three-block area. I heard a jungle of noises over the phone, then the sound of a man's breath before Bill spoke.

"You've got a pair calling me here."

"Don't sweat it. Officer Geritol is outside. I'm calling about your friend."

"Speak to Jimmy?"

"I did."

"I'm impressed."

"Not as impressed as I was with the welcome party I received at your friend's place."

I let that sink in. Welcome party was military parlance for a beat-down from the instructor cadre. Ahead of me, I spotted a working girl and her pimp. She might've wanted breakfast and he seemed to improvise on the slogan for a cereal commercial, "Silly bitch, breakfast is for kids." She was wearing a long coat and not much else underneath. He was styling black cords for slacks, a turtleneck as long as a neck brace, and a mink coat. Every day was Halloween in this town. "You okay?" I heard in my ear.

A police cruiser rolled by and I angled my profile so the cops couldn't see my face.

"Yeah," I said. "Thanks for asking. I've got some bruises to share with you. Look, I need something from you. Pen and paper?"

"Hold on." I heard movement. "Shoot."

"I need an address and a pedigree on a mutt."

"Name and description?"

"Name is Dunbar, he's five-four, late forties to mid-fifties, and has no distinguishing marks or features." I threw in eye and hair color. "Try Daniel for a first name, though I think it's a wash. Got all that?"

"Got it. Should I call you later, say, six o'clock at your office?"

"Don't bother," I said. "I'll find you at your usual place. Still hang there, don't you?"

Bill was young, good looking, a combat-decorated veteran, and a great cop with one unfortunate problem: he was so deep in the closet he blended in with the scent of mothballs.

"Yeah, I socialize there," he said. "Shane?"

"What?"

"I responded to a 10-65, and I've got a feeling about this case."

"You have a feeling about a dead body?" I asked. Bill chewed on my ear about a woman, strangled in her apartment. He was first on the scene and the first to notify Homicide. Morbid as it sounded, Bill was delighted as a student who had peeked at the surprise quiz inside the teacher's desk. His intuition said she had been murdered by her soon-to-be ex-husband. Divorce papers had been filed, he added, but never processed. No preliminaries for COD from the ME yet, but it didn't take a Medical Examiner to see the woman had had the life choked out of her.

Bill went on and on, about the layout of the scene, how the place reeked of cigarette smoke and how she was fresh out of the shower, her hair still wet. He said he identified the shampoo by scent. Breck. He confirmed what his nose knew with a visit to her bathroom. I could hear the excitement in Bill's voice, my little Encyclopedia Brown. I took a chisel to his enthusiasm to give him focus.

"Start with the husband," I said. "The spouse is always the first suspect until you can rule him out." I didn't want to seem abrupt, so I indulged him. "What can you tell me about him?"

"Some ROs on him, but he's never violated a Restraining Order, and the guys at the station told me a woman intent on divorce will often cite abuse for the court's sympathy and the fat alimony check. But the thing is, there are no kids. I've pulled the jacket on this guy and read the statements from friends and family. The dude is a walking commercial for Summer's Eve."

"The guy's a douche, I get it, but you either make the case or rule him out. And do yourself a favor, Bill…" I paused for emphasis. "Don't listen to the cynics at the office."

"Any other advice?"

"Rigor mortis sets in two-to-six hours after death, and you know what state the body was in when you found it, so work backwards from there because the ME's report will take days."

"Got it, start a timeline," he said, confident and motivated.

"Sketch it all out on the QT, and steer clear of the suits in Homicide. Politics and personalities. We'll talk later."

I hung up.

***

I made it to my office with other thoughts on my mind. I had slept with my paycheck and I hated myself for it.

No, I didn't.

Yeah, I did.

I had compromised my integrity and my objectivity, if such a thing ever existed with Cat. Our particular history read more like push and pull, rough and smooth. We shouldn't work at all, but like sweet and sour, it did when we paired up. The thing is, Cat was always able to walk away from me.

She had her mother's blue blood and daddy's appetite for the good things in life. Pedigree and prestige, the other pride and prejudice. Related to most of New England's upper crust, those dour and imperious faces found in dim oil paintings that hung in museums, she had no money until she married Bray.

Delilah jumped up on the blotter as I leaned back in the chair, feet up on the desk. Her nose sniffed about before she eased back on her haunches in judgment. Her nose twitched with disapproval and I saw her blink.

"Don't you start with me," I said.

She stared back at me. Her tail curled around her white pillowcase feet. Then her tail moved. I watched the tip of that tail lift and thump down like a gavel. She fixed her gaze on me the whole time and let me work myself over. I considered the far wall.

Cat, my former love and latest fling, intoxicated me. Cat was both angel and demon, my heaven and hell. She was also somebody else's wife. I tilted my head and contemplated the ceiling, its smooth polar surface. Delilah's unremitting stare continued. She had not moved. She had not wavered. "Are you Catholic or what?" I asked her.

She mewed.

"It was wrong. I know that."

She squeaked.

"Fine, stay angry and hold a grudge."

I had tried to make good with Delilah. I shook the kibble bag. Nothing. I slow-cranked the can opener on her favorite wet food. Nothing. I doled out a generous portion of it onto a clean plate. I set the dish down on the hardwood floor.

I watched her turn away. She gave me the hindmost view and jumped down to the floor.

***

I showered and changed at the gym. Cat's scent disappeared down the drain, but drifted around inside my head with the steam, locked and stored for immediate recall. My Catholic upbringing offered infinite ways for me to torment myself.

I stopped to watch two men in the ring on my way out. If I had known I was frustrated about Cat I could have come here and been smart about my stupidity. I could've worked her out of my system, taken a beating instead of the one I inflicted on myself. I missed the smell of leather, the righteous sweat and most of all, landing a perfect combination to KO my opponent. There's no greater joy than taped hands, twelve-ounce gloves on, the tat-tat-tat rhythm of the speed ball, or the creak of the chains above the heavy bag as it moved with punches that connected.

I stayed for a few rounds to watch two fighters.

The writer A.J. Liebling called boxing the Sweet Science. He was right. There at ringside, as I watched these two, I was reminded that boxing was a brutal and honest metaphor for life itself. You could use all your best footwork to avoid the inevitable fight, like this guy in front of me seemed to be doing, or you could engage, absorb some blows and land a few.

The more I watched them, the more I realized I had been wrong about the dancer in the ring. He was sizing up his opponent. The jabs here and there he used as tests. Like a doctor, he assessed and diagnosed, observed how the man in front of him moved and reacted. I saw it in his eyes, the concentration. I'd done it myself numerous times.

No matter how many times I'd sit down with my old man on Friday nights for the Gillette Fight of the Week, the camera never picked up certain nuances in a boxer's eyes. Me and the old man would yell at our Zenith. He'd throw his popcorn at the television screen, and I swept up the kernels after the match.

The sweet science.

Science was life and death, the intervals of give and take, pain and pleasure, the ways in which you learned about yourself in victory or defeat. Therein lies the beauty of an ugly sport. Someone won and someone lost, and odds were both men left bruised and battered. Boxing was physical and mental. People could talk all they wanted about reach, about height, about a glass jaw, or who had the hardest head, and the heaviest punch, but it mattered little. The man who fell and refused to stay down was the one you respected. He haunted you.

The bell rang. In their respective corners, the boxers received advice from their cornermen. They nodded in understanding of the next round's strategy. They swished water in their mouths, spat into buckets. Mouthpieces jammed in, they returned to the fight, to life itself.

The gym here was no Boston Garden.

My dad took me to see Tony DeMarco battle Johnny Saxon for the welterweight title. DeMarco, a Sicilian from the North End, slugged it out for twelve rounds before he won the belt in '55. Twenty years ago, I saw them with my father. We watched Demarco pummel Saxton with every combination until the ref stopped the fight and declared a TKO.

Same year, we watched DeMarco fight Carmen Basilio. Twice. The first time on television, televised from Syracuse. The second time, we had tickets to the match at The Garden.

Tony lost both times, but those two bouts against Basilio were Fights of the Year. The crowd at The Garden hushed when DeMarco leveled Basilio with a left hook in the seventh round. A wicked punch, as Boston's true sons call it. Basilio earned my respect, and the crowd's admiration because he stood his ground. His knees trembled but he wouldn't fall. I watched him use his left foot to stamp the crack to the chin out before he returned for the eighth round. Tony may have lost in the twelfth round again, but he made Boston proud.

The Commonwealth can boast of a long lineage of men in the ring. Marciano hailed from Brockton, both 'Skeeter' McClure and 'Sandy' Saddler were from Boston proper—hell, you could turn the pages back to John L.

Sullivan, who came from Roxbury. Matches may have been fought in Fenway Park, but The Garden was where any boxer worth his spit wanted to fight.

My father took me there several times. I remembered odors most. Cigarette and cigar smoke rose like a fog and shone under the lights above the ring. My mother said I reeked for days. Cigar smoke clung to everything. And those lights were stark and bright as a searchlight over the dark sea of suits and dresses. Everyone wore their second Sunday best clothes. I could pick out the gangsters because of their loud ties, double-breasted suits and pinky rings. Their molls hung off their arms in fitted dresses so tight you'd think they'd lose them with one good fart. Girls announced each round with large placards, doing the catwalk around the ring in bikinis. Sportswriters in the pit worked typewriter keys like hopped-up jazz pianists so their coverage of the fight made it into the morning edition. Photographers circled the ropes and seeded themselves in the corners, ready with their Graflexes. After the fight, the floor crunched from hundreds of bulbs crushed underfoot. Nobody cared. I tasted my first beer at The Garden.

A thud interrupted my reverie. The guy who danced before, the clinician I thought was the better man in the fight? He was kissing the canvas.

Boxing was like that. Life was like that. The unexpected happened.

I checked my watch.

Time to visit Bill, but first I wanted a change of clothes to match the nightlife and Bill's social scene. I headed back to the office, where I put on a fresh shirt, a pullover sweater over it, jeans and a holster clip to the right of my tailbone for variety this time. I opted for a pair of boots. Cuban boots were back in style. When she heard the jingle of the keys, Delilah rushed my feet. She tapped my pant leg several times with her paw.

"Now you want to talk? You had your chance."

Chapter 9: Bonfires to Light

Bill frequented a bar off of Park Plaza. There's not a lot there, except old blood and bad history. The most respectable citizen in the neighborhood was the last hotel Ellsworth Milton Statler built before he checked out in 1928. The country's father of hotels had purchased a parcel of land that formed a triangle at Providence Street, Commonwealth Avenue, and Arlington Street. His hotel was two-faced, with its western side composed of rooms for guests, while the eastern half provided offices. Once the second tallest structure in Boston, it was the back yard to strip clubs, topless bars, and adult bookshops and theaters.

There was talk of R&R, renovation and revitalization, in certain quarters of business and government, but it came to nothing because of too much talk, too much money, and too many memories of folks booted from the West End, their property razed. And then there was the lingering stench from the fire at the Cocoanut Grove at Providence street that killed more than 400 people two days after Thanksgiving in 1942.

I thought I'd take a shortcut through one of the side-alleys. Shortcuts don't go unrewarded in this life. I learned that lesson at St. Wystan's from Homer's Odysseus who had taken the ten-year detour to feed his ego and carnal appetites, and I was about to learn it again when two swarthy types ambushed me. Assault was a more accurate word. These weren't muggers or thugs interested in my pocket change, or out for the thrill of rolling a drunk, or hooligans on a Fag Hunt.

"Had to stick it to Douglas, didn't you, Cleary?"

The first blow crimped my stomach and folded me in two. I braced for the next barrage of fists. A question raced through my head. Were these two connected to my uninvited guest in Bay Village, or was this simply karma with compounded interest? Set aside their opener about Douglas, their shoes said these two were fresh off-the-clock cops.

"Just couldn't leave it alone, could ya," one of them said after he kneed me. The other asked, "What you gotta say for yourself?"

I answered him. "Go spit on a snowflake."

"Wiseguy."

I tried to guard my face like a boxer. I tried. They hoisted me upright against the masonry behind me to work my midsection. They tried. I have a strong spine and they couldn't straighten it. I hugged the sidewalk, soft as snow, while they made like shovels and kicked me.

"Hey there!" a voice thundered and I saw the blur of a silhouette ahead of me. Bill?

"Mind your own business, bud," one of my attackers yelled.

"I don't think I will." I heard next that welcome sound, a shotgun being chambered. The feet in front of me disappeared fast.

I stood up, back against the bricks. Face intact, I breathed through the correct orifices. I checked my ribs and my hip for my .38. I said my name to myself. Cleary was as Irish as O'Reilly. I recited my social, blood type, and religious denomination, as if Mortuary were reading my dog tag before they stuffed me inside a pouch. The sensitive boys at the Pentagon insisted that nobody called them body bags.

"You okay?"

"Yeah," I said. "Let's hope those boys didn't recognize you."

"Friendship with you is a gift."

"Thanks. Now a favor from you."

"Sure."

"Sit and spin," I said and gave him the finger.

Bill must've seen us from his car. He mentioned something to that effect, and said he recruited the shotgun from his trunk. Good thing.

I enjoyed the cold stinging air. Odd memories of St. Wystan's bolted through my mind during the beatdown. Nuns and priests, timetables for classes, the chores before breakfast, dinner, and bedtime. Church. I had attended enough Masses at St. Wystan's to earn the respect of a medieval monk.

"Thanks again, Bill. I owe you."

"Famous last words, right?"

I put a hand on my hip. The .38 was there. I pointed to Bill's shotgun. "Let's get Betsy back to bed inside your car."

***

I followed Bill, anxious to escape the frigid night. There was six feet of corridor, and the promise of music in the distance. I passed two guys pressed against the wall. One had his back to me, hands not his own working his back pockets. His partner, pressed against the wall, came up for air, rested his chin on his friend's shoulder and winked at me. I saw wet glass for eyes before the face dived down for more kisses. I knew that look.

Each club had its calling card, its drug. Bill let me in on what and where. On any given night you could score your pharmacopeia of choice.

Downers. LSD and mescaline. Quaaludes, and a variety of uppers.

At a club on Lansdowne Street, Bill and I once watched a guy, over our martinis, drop into the K-hole of ketamine while the soundtrack to *Mary Poppins* blared from speakers.

Bill's taste in men was eclectic, though I was never certain with whom he was intimate or whom he rated as a mere acquaintance. I assumed Bill was sorting out whom and what he liked. I knew drugs weren't Bill's scene, and that winnowed down prospects in the boudoir.

I had tagged along with Bill once or twice. Social calls, as he called them. I've met all the boys. Crazy Carlos, a short guy who talked so fast that coffee calmed him down. There was Wayne, a giant. He walked around with a small Tiffany bottle on a chain around his neck so he could snort a whiff any time he wanted his high. Amyl Nitrate Wayne.

Bill moved with confidence. This bar was familiar territory to him. Bill let the bouncer know I was with him. That saved me the frisk. The barkeep, a cue ball with a serious case of black eyeliner, gave me the eye as he stretched forward with a rag to clean his precious counter. Music played, but not so loud that we had to scream to talk.

The owner waved. Bill said the guy knew he was a cop. We sat on the far side of the room in a horseshoe booth so we could eye the door.

"What have you got for me on Dunbar?" I asked.

He produced a piece of paper and pushed it forward. "First name is Nathaniel."

"Not too far off from Daniel," I said and asked about aliases, and priors.

"Nope and nope, although he's a vet. Korea. Honorably discharged and separated as an O-2."

I noticed Bill was chewing gum. I scanned his report while he checked out the scenery. I somehow had a home address for Dunbar. I didn't ask how, since Dunbar didn't drive. Bill tapped his fingers on the table, to the beat of the music.

An O-2 was a first lieutenant and that meant a college degree. Bill's jaw tensed while he chewed and his head did the goose to the beat. "Anything else, Bill?"

"Man is Mr. Clean minus the bald head, white shirt, and biceps."

"Any chance Mr. Clean has a weapon registered in his good name?"

I got the nope refrain. A crowd formed on the oak parquet dance-floor. Big Five financial-types entered stage left, tie knots pulled loose, and mustachioed Marlboro men in red plaid shirts and tight denims eyed them like Jets who spotted a herd of Sharks. The music wasn't Leonard Bernstein. Some biker boys in leather filled out this odd rodeo. A suit preened by. His eyes had taken a fast Polaroid of Bill. I sat there as out of place as the spinster aunt asked to chaperone the first Sadie Hawkins dance of the year.

The world had changed, and would keep on changing, whether I liked it or not, whether I understood it or not. I never understood Bill's world, the relationships. Mostly sex. I was lucky to have great parents, unlucky to lose them too soon. I never understood why my father killed himself. My mother was lost after he died. All I understood was that life was harder on her, on most women. Divorce left them alone in the world, and the death of a husband, lonelier. My world turned. I got it.

Students protested Vietnam. Women Libbers demonstrated against inequality. Blacks clenched their fists. Queers rebelled after Stonewall, and here I was in a queer club with a friend, a fellow veteran, but it all seemed strange to me.

"Anything you want from me, or can I go have some fun now?" Bill asked.

"One thing."

"Shoot."

"Hear any good gossip in this part of the world?"

"All the time. Be more specific," he answered, hand up for a waiter. Bill wanted a drink, and I could use one after the interlude outside. Something to comfort and yet smack me.

"Real estate deals. Hot investments?"

A shirtless Boy Wonder appeared in chaps, his shoulders broad enough to block out the sun. His sandy hair was feathered back and he sported an inexplicable tan in December. His physique was an anatomical chart that could've walked off a classroom wall. He had a pad and pen in hand and a bow tie around his neck.

"What can I get you, boys?"

"G & T, please," Bill said.

"And what about you, sir?"

"Bourbon neat."

The scratches I heard on the pad reminded me of the waitresses at the diner with Lindsey. I tried to ignore how the chaps framed the man's bottom like an apple as he walked away. Some images I don't want, or need inside my head at 3 a.m. when I question my existence.

"Bourbon?" Bill said. "How butch of you."

"For the record, I don't like ordering drinks in bars. Ever hear of a Mickey Finn."

"Yeah, I dated him once. Relax," Bill said. "I know the owner, remember?"

Like that purchased any consolation for me. I queried again. "No chatter about prime real estate about to come on the market?" Bill seemed distracted with all the candy in the room. "Bill? Hear anything?"

"Jesus, you won't let up, will you? I'm off the clock."

"I'm not," I said.

"I might have heard something, but c'mon, I can't weigh every crumb." I stared at him and he relented. "A fling told me some big money types were interested in waterfront property. Usual quick get-rich talk. I doubt what he said was on the level."

"Why not?" I asked.

"The guy lives in East Boston and is a scrub at Merrill Lynch."

"When E.F. Hutton talks, people—"

"When E.F. Hutton wants to get laid, he'll say anything. Although, come to think of it, he mentioned something about highways as part of this blockbuster deal."

"Highways? The mayor tried that once and it got him nothing but grief."

"This guy is nowhere near connected to City Hall, that I can assure you," Bill said.

I did some thinking while Bill's eyes cruised the landscape. Mayor Kevin White tried to muster interest in a super-highway. He commissioned a presentation and went so far as to name the proposal Innovation District, but it died a lonely death in the end. There was some work done, but construction sputtered, stuttered, and stopped.

"Here you go, boys," our waiter said. He set down the napkins first and then our drinks. He did it with panache. I dug into my pocket and paid our tab. I told him to keep the change. "Why thank you, sir," he said and his fingers lingered on mine. I didn't think of myself as old enough to warrant 'sir.'

"Did your friend mention any names or companies?" I asked Bill.

"What difference would it make? Guy was a grope in the dark months ago." Bill's tone of voice suggested annoyance. I detected a smidge of jealousy after the attention I received from the waiter.

"I don't get it," Bill said.

"Get what?"

"Your questions and Dunbar."

"Working an angle. What else did your scrub from East Boston say?"

"Told you." Bill's hand came down like a tomahawk. "Something about a thoroughfare from Boston out to the waterfront. Some kind of artery, or something."

66

"Artery?" I said, as my hand's warmth coaxed the whiskey to body temperature. "The pols have yapped about connecting North and South Stations, but that never happened."

"Aren't you the optimist?" he said while he flirted with a dancer on the floor.

"I'm a realist. Land development involves money, kickbacks, cronyism and nepotism."

I took my first mouthful of bourbon, thinking of Brayton and Cat, the odd couple.

Bill turned in his seat, headlights for eyes on me, and G&T in his grip. "I'd like to talk about Roger."

"Didn't find him in Bay Village. Sorry."

"What did Jimmy say?"

"He explained Roger's line of work to me, and he said you knew about it, but neglected to tell me."

"Does it matter?" Bill asked.

I kicked him softly under the table. "It matters when a cop tried to pulp me."

"I'm sorry I didn't tell you. But I didn't know how you'd feel about that kind of thing."

"It's called motive, Bill. You're more worried what I think about sex parties than sending me for a cleaning and dental work?"

I had offended him. Bill, drink in hand, started his exit from the horseshoe. I grabbed his arm. "Sit back down. I'm sorry. I'm working two cases at once. Is there any chance this Nathaniel guy is, you know?"

"Is what, Shane? Queer? You seriously think I can tell from a piece of paper?"

"He squeaks clean, Bill. I can almost hear the windshield wipers against the glass."

"It may come as a shock to you, Shane Cleary, but there are all kinds of people in this world. They work, they pay taxes and some live dull and uneventful lives."

"C'mon," I said. "Let's review the facts. Nathaniel is older and unmarried.

He has no discernible life to speak of, other than military service. You mean to tell me that you can live half a century and don't so much as leave a smudge somewhere, anywhere? It's not impossible, but unlikely is all I'm saying."

Bill sipped his G&T. "Boring don't make him queer."

I drank my bourbon and decided to drop the queer bit. I couldn't care less what Dunbar did in his bedroom. As for Officer Bill, Boston wasn't so enlightened, and the BPD believed in black and white, and extremes in politics. Either JFK was a saint or a communist. There was no middle road.

"Any chance your partner knew I was headed to Bay Village?" I asked. "Say anything, even if it was unintentional and innocent? Think hard for me, Bill."

"I didn't say a word. Not one."

"He saw us, Bill. He could've dropped a dime when you weren't looking."

"He didn't. I'm positive of that."

"How can you be so sure?" I asked.

The music was building to a crescendo, and the lighting changed as a mirrored ball descended from the ceiling. Small squares of light swirled around the room, flooding the floor. Thoughts, like a storm inside a snow globe, swirled inside my head, and I needed more than Bill's word. Moments and music passed before Bill spoke.

"Looks are deceiving, aren't they?" he said.

"What the hell are you talking about"

"Officer Geritol is older, never married, and has no life to speak of."

"Oh?" I said. "Oh," I repeated, surprised, before I took in the last of the bourbon.

"He's terrified someone will find out."

There was my explanation as to why the old-timer chose Bill for his twilight walk into retirement. I hadn't seen that at all. Talk about revelations of the Biblical kind. I thought back to Dunbar and Cat while the whiskey worked through my veins. Fifty-grand per page was bold, and yet Dunbar broke a sweat and checked his watch about how long he took for a smoke in the lounge. That's too much conscience for blackmail. I should talk about conscience. I cashiered the last of my good name on my desk with Cat. Bill's partner hadn't leaked our meeting on Summer Street to his buddies in blue, but a cop did greet me at Roger's place, and two others worked my ribs like a xylophone outside in Park Plaza.

Bill's report gave me an address for Dunbar.

Jimmy had given me the name Marty Savitz.

Braddock claimed blackmail would sink his ship, but it seemed to me his moneyed friends could afford to weather setbacks and, from the sound of it, this enhancement they had planned for Boston would get done one way or the other.

Part curiosity, part desire to pay Bill back for the favor, I asked about the homicide that piqued his detective skills. He relayed details unavailable or unrealized since he started his investigation. He had smelled cigarette smoke, but her place was clean for cigarettes. He told me that the lead on the case filed a request with the Insurance Board to determine if she had life insurance and whether the husband was the beneficiary. That ate up time, like the autopsy would.

"Any signs of an SOS?" I asked.

"A distress signal?"

"No, signs of sex. Independent of the Restraining Order, did she seek out help? Women talk to each other, so find a girlfriend or a neighbor."

Bill hammered the point that he'd blow his cover if he canvassed friends, family, and the neighborhood. He reminded me that the two detectives had conducted interviews, and I reminded him that they were checking off the boxes while sleepwalking.

"Their first priority was Summer's Eve, Bill."

"I'm confused. Didn't you tell me the same thing? Start with the douche. You specifically said, establish a timeline, or have you forgotten?"

"I didn't forget, Bill. Yes, work out the timeline, but do what I'm doing, and work two cases. You say they canvassed the neighborhood?"

He told me they had talked with neighbors, upstairs and downstairs.

"Nothing says you can't follow-up," I said. "Talk to the lady across the way, or somebody with a view to a window." He looked at me as if I had watched Hitchcock one time too many. "Didn't you tell me these dicks didn't care about her?"

"Did I say that?" Bill pulled his head back, doubting himself.

"You implied it when you told me that the detectives in Homicide said women headed for divorce court beef up their case with allegations of domestic abuse. Anything to fatten the purse and alimony check. Remember?"

"I remember. Your point?"

"That attitude says they don't give a shit about her, and they're doing this case by the book with a loose binding. My point is, work the timeline on the jerk, but do something else for her because the suits in Homicide don't give a damn about her. Got it?"

I scooched out of the horseshoe. I told Bill that I'd be in touch if I had any news on Roger. I wanted to see what came of Jimmy's lead first, Savitz, before I proceeded with Bray's blackmail case.

I waded through flesh and some unwelcome hands on my person. I empathized with women after I inhaled more than a dozen colognes and aftershaves on my way out. The bar was turning positively lavender and I had a lead to investigate, while these upstanding gentlemen, whatever their lineage or profession might be, had their bonfires to light this winter's eve.

Chapter 10: One of The Regulars

Kenmore Square. Turnover was high, crime frequent, though the Square retained a distinctive bohemian air. Students came and went, on the move for a cheap meal and a cheaper room. This was where the Sox fans in their home-team colors of red-and-white overran Fenway Park like redcoats on Game Day against the reviled New York Yankees.

Every city has its sign, its icon, and for Boston it's the CITGO sign, a red triangle on a white background on top of the Peerless Building. Silent sentinel by day, and both beacon of light and character actor at night, the skyline feature worked the night-shift from eight to midnight during Red Sox games. As I exited the T-station's subterranean tunnel to get on the other side of the street to Marty Savitz's office inside the Hotel Charlesview, I heard the screech of a Green Line trolley car behind me and the rumbling of the 57 bus ahead of me. Cars of all sorts fed Beacon Street and Brookline Ave. I heard another noise now. Grandpa Walton in a wood-paneled station wagon jammed on the brakes and yelled at the kid in the intersection.

College kids were everywhere. Kids from Grahm Junior College, kids from Boston University, and kids in all forms of adolescent statements of protest crisscrossed in front of me. A tough with a black eye and sallow face from last night's bender did his best to stare me down.

My eyes fixed on a green jacket. I tried to discern the flash on the sleeve, but it was nothing more than a surplus item from the Army-Navy store. Out of the converted properties from yesteryear flowed students who should be grateful they weren't drafted. A few short years ago I was their age, fighting for my life in a far-away place, wearing a poncho. A young man with the latest vinyl from the record store tucked under his arm was jawing the vernacular about a band at The Rat last night. A pair of attractive girls discussed their dates and their plans for a Guinness float at the Deli Haus tonight.

A cup and the jingle of song disrupted the postcard I was reading in the crowd around me. I looked up and found a tall black man in Rasta dreads, a pleasant smile on his face, the guitar strap across his chest like a bandolier. The *chuk-chuk* of his nickels and dimes stopped. He announced me when our eyes met.

"Here comes one of the regulars."

My hand inside my pocket, I asked him if he wanted change for coffee.

"Naw, man. I'm collecting taxes."

I folded a George Washington and sank it into his cup. "For the tax increase," I told him.

"That's too much, man, but I'd take some grass if you have any."

"So would I," I answered.

He returned to the rhythm of coins in a cup, while I finished recon. Marty Savitz kept an office in a professional building, if professional meant the tenants included drifters and fortune-tellers, although I did see a legitimate dry cleaner and a hair salon. The property had fallen on hard times from its heyday as a hotel. Marty must've been grandfathered into his lease when the rents dropped and the local color and crime increased. Drug deals in plain sight took place often. *The Herald* ramped up their articles on raids for narcotics, stabbings, and shootings to scare voters into voting for Law and Order during election season.

I pulled on a heavy front door, all the heavier with the winter wind at my back. The faint smell of Pine-Sol greeted me in the hallway. An elevator promised to lift me up and away. No security guard stopped me and dingy lettering on the wall told me where I'd find my destination.

I got off the lift on the fourth floor. Down the shabby, ill-lit hallway I walked, hearing nothing but the click-clack of a lone typewriter. A fluorescent rod overhead flickered, undecided whether it wanted to live and stay lit, or die because nothing mattered in this godforsaken tunnel. I counted the number of brittle carapaces of cockroaches trapped inside the fixture. Five too many. I knocked on a walnut door with the man's name and specialty in gold leaf and black trim.

"Come in," a feminine voice said.

She was the source of the long-and-short staccato sounds in my journey. She sat behind a desk made of dark imitation wood, her hands intent on the communiqué beneath her fingertips. The wall behind her displayed clients from all the local teams: New England Patriots, Boston Red Sox, the Celtics, and the Bruins. Some PawSoxs, minor-league baseball players, were relegated to a small corner near a potted ficus. I browsed all the beaming faces, ignored the autographed endearments, while Miss Distressed clattered away. A fortress of paperwork bordered one side of her blotter.

"Shane Cleary," I said, without eliciting so much as a tremor from her eyelashes. "Calling on Marty Savage."

"It's Savitz. Do you have an appointment, Mr. Cleary?"

"No appointment."

"Mr. Savitz doesn't do walk-ins."

"He'd appreciate talking to me before the Boston Police Department does."

"With regards to what?"

"Roger Sherman."

"Wait one moment, please," she said. A thin hand snatched the receiver. I had already seen the shadow flit by the glass door behind her. Savitz had the quiet feet of a cat and probably the hearing of one, too.

"You can go in now, Mr. Cleary."

Her eyes returned to the captive sheet of paper trapped around the roller inside the blue chunk of metal IBM called the Selectric II. As the doorknob turned, I heard rapid keystrokes that reminded me of an M16.

"Come on in, Mr. Cleary."

The room was large and square, the windows with a view of Kenmore Square were meant to impress. My feet dragged through shag carpeting. The décor suggested solid and dependable, but the shades of brown reminded me of the dead insects earlier. The pristine and streak-free windows in the office impressed me because they were pristine and streak-free. The man came at me with his extended hand for a greeting.

"Marty Savitz. How do you do?"

A hefty man in red velour pants, a shirt with enlarged paramecia for a pattern, and western boots stood in front of me. I've seen a better wardrobe in a stag film.

"My secretary mentioned Roger Sherman. How can I help?"

I tried not to stare at the thick rope of gold chain around his neck, or the Hebrew letter there. His collar was spread coast to coast, from one shoulder to the other, and exposed a nest of chest hair.

"Have you seen him recently?" I asked the sports agent.

"About two weeks ago?"

"Not more recently?"

"Not that I recall. Why do you ask?"

Inconclusive and noncommittal to either lies or truth, Marty Savitz was experienced in evasive maneuvers. Only screenwriters and suspense writers answered a question with a question. He was clean-shaven, slapped twice with Aramis cologne, and ready to take down the toughest used-car salesman.

"Nothing really," I said. "A client of mine wishes to discuss a personal matter with Mr. Sherman, but can't seem to find him."

"Discuss what with him?"

"I'd rather not say," I said. "Is he a client of yours?"

"Mr. Sherman is not an athlete," he said with a paternal hand on my shoulder and a pretend fit of laughter. He moved fast to his next statement. "I would've thought your client would've told you that. You do know his line of business, don't you?"

"I'm just following where the trail leads me, Mr. Savitz. And yes, I'm aware Mr. Sherman is not in professional sports, though, like my client, he is fond of hockey. A Bruins fan."

His feelers for eyebrows twitched. I wanted to keep him on the ropes. "Would you happen to represent any players from the team?" His mouth moved to answer, but I cut him off. "Of course you do, I saw your wall outside, behind your secretary." I walked around him. "Some view you've got here." I stood near the window long enough for the traffic light down below to change.

"I wish I could help you, Mr. Cleary, but I've neither seen nor heard from Mr. Sherman." The light clap of his hands would've signaled the conclusion of our meeting, but I waited for him to take the bait I dropped in front of his secretary.

"Did I hear something about the police?"

"Oh, that's all right, Mr. Savitz," I said. "Don't concern yourself with them. You said so yourself that you haven't seen or heard from him, and that's good enough for me. I'll tell my client he should expect Mr. Sherman at the next social."

"What social?"

I moved in, the way an officer approached a recruit, a breath away from his eyes, and said, "The next sports night. Thanks for your time, Mr. Savitz. I'll show myself out."

Two steps away, I heard, "May I have your business card in the event I do hear from Mr. Sherman? For your client's sake."

"Certainly." I reached into my pocket and faked an embarrassed smile. "How irresponsible of me and thoughtful of you to ask."

He read my card on his way to his desk. "Allow me to return the favor and give you my card, Mr. Cleary. Feel free to call me at any time, day or night. I also have an answering service."

His card was as I expected it: high-end stock, elegant typeset. I thanked him and closed the door to his office behind me.

I glimpsed a better look at his secretary this time. She wore no makeup except a touch of gloss on nice lips. Her eyes were a shade of brown, lighter than her eyebrows but darker than her hair. She seemed sick of long hallways that led nowhere, sick of earth tones and Aramis, sick and afraid that the highlight of her career was Marty Savitz and the ledge in his office wasn't high enough from the street. I picked up the nameplate on her desk.

"Ms. E. Cummings. Your last name is Cummings, as in the poet."

"E is for Elizabeth."

"Well, Elizabeth. I hope you have a nice day."

"Thank you, Mr. Cleary. It's been a long time since someone's called me

Elizabeth."

"You must have some friends."

"Not really. I work all the time."

"Family?"

"Deceased."

At the door to the hallway, I turned around and she looked up. "Yes?"

"Call me Shane, if there is a next time."

***

I ambled to the Store-24 instead of the IHOP for a dose of caffeine and a newspaper. I worked the dispenser for my cup of black coffee, wrestled a lid onto my Styrofoam cup. I saw a copy of *The Boston Globe*. The headline said something inflammatory about wasted taxpayers' money. I read the first page last. I was more curious about the latest advice in the "Ask Beth" column. I stepped to the counter where I found the Rasta paying the clerk for my Joe and paper. Surprised by this unexpected generosity, I said, "Thank you, sir."

"Please, don't call me sir. I work for a living." I smiled at the old Army joke about the difference between officers and grunts. "Thanks then," I said.

"You're welcome. Consider it an early tax refund."

Chapter 11: Nap Time

Bill's research said Dunbar lived on Beacon Hill, a few blocks away from the Braddocks.

My right ventricle should've clamped shut as I bit into my dinner of Buzzy's roast beef there under the Charles Street train stop. I wish I'd chosen the knishes and BBQ sauce instead of the signature shop sandwich. Spicy mustard burned the corners of my mouth. I didn't order pastrami because I couldn't betray Henry Bauman in Cambridge. His hand-cut extra-thick pastrami, served hot on a bulky roll, was worth a walk in a blizzard to Mt. Auburn Street in Harvard Square. An Elsie Meal Card sat behind my PI license in my wallet. The train rumbled overhead. The outbound Red Line to Cambridge rattled like a rollercoaster doing the dry heave up a steep incline.

With the slur of cars in the street in front of me, drunks behind me, the Charles Street Jail at an angle from where I stood, I had to decide which of the steep streets I would climb for my destination on Beacon Hill. Joy Street was not my first choice. Emphasis on *not*. Runners in tracksuits used the pavement there as a fitness test. The cardiac ward of Mass General was across the street for them.

Beacon Hill was Skid Row for every skunk lawyer and slippery politician in the Commonwealth. I've seen bulbous-nosed shysters take the stairs down to basement bars for their morning aperitif. I've watched Ciceronian con men in striped ties hold court at other gentrified saloons. I've heard all thirty-two brogues of foreign-born Irishmen. I've had pizza at the stardust counter in the only Italian pizzeria on the Hill. I've picked up laundry from the one Chinaman's dry-cleaning store, but asking me to believe that a bean counter could afford an apartment in these woods was like asking me to believe the Sox had a chance of breaking The Curse of the Bambino and winning the World Series.

I stared down the long barrel of his street. A mist of rain was falling, uncertain if it wanted to turn into snow or sleet. Cobblestones glistened under the lampposts. I smelled wood smoke in the air. It was a scent that conjured up memories of home, hearth, and Jimmy Stewart as George Bailey. I imagined a wee lad with a perfect arm on his bike at 6 a.m., throwing newspapers that hit the mark every time with a slap, his route done by 6:30. At precisely 7:15, wives up and down this lane would open their front doors, robes knotted, and wave goodbye in unison to their brood of adorable children. The sigh escaped their collective lips at 7:17. At this hour of the night, though, the dishes were in the dishwasher and the husband had nodded off. His frustrated wife stared at the television, and imagined she has committed some heinous crime in San Francisco, so Michael Douglas as Inspector Keller will cuff her and take her away from it all, and she'll swoon every step of the way.

I checked the number.

I had been misled. Bill may've written "apartment" but this was a townhouse, likely a meetinghouse for abolitionists in the last century. I put my face to a square of windowpane and confirmed it for myself. I could live and die in the receiving parlor. I pressed a button and an angelus bell announced my presence.

Dunbar, in a spotted silk robe, opened the door the required two inches for politeness, peering over the linked chain. His eyes did a slow up-and-down on my person. I smiled and told him I was alone. I heard the scratch of the chain, after which the door widened. I stepped in.

"What a surprise. I wasn't expecting you, Mr. Fletcher."

The scent of strong coffee met my nose. He offered to take my coat. I said I wouldn't be staying long. He said we should talk. I agreed. He suggested the parlor. I wanted to ask which one, but didn't. I told him he ought to fetch his coffee. I didn't want any when he asked. Whatever or whoever Dunbar was, he had manners. He asked me to follow him.

We traveled a hall into the kitchen. Original paintings hung in frames fit for a museum. I didn't stop to read the little brass plaques. He poured himself coffee, offered me a mug again. I declined.

We walked down another hall, turned a corner into a dark room. A fireplace flickered and a small Tiffany lamp for reading shed light. He sat down in an armchair. To his right he rested his coffee on a coaster and to the left, on a smallish stand, he had a long book opened. A pair of glasses rested in the crease. He pointed me to the Queen Anne sofa. "Have a seat," he said.

"I didn't recall you wearing glasses," I said.

"Only when I work. I hide them otherwise. Vanity."

"And what kind of work is that, if I may cut to the chase?"

"I should ask you the same question, Mr. Fletcher, or is it Mr. Cleary?"

"It's Shane, Nathaniel."

He smiled at that. We had settled up on our pretenses. I watched him sip coffee. He reached for his glasses. I would have chosen smaller frames, but they did become him. The Oriental rug was real and vintage. If Henry James were correct about rugs, the fireplace should reveal figures in the pattern. I considered the walls. The wainscoting was impressive, as were the moldings. Fresh-cut flowers jammed into a crystal vase sat next to a small tragic statue.

"I wasn't lying," he said.

"About which part?"

"About being a consultant."

"I wasn't either," I said.

It was cold, it was December, and neither of us seemed interested in a game of tennis or chess. I unbuttoned my jacket, but not to reveal my .38. I did cross a leg, to show I wore socks. Glasses or no glasses, Dunbar didn't miss a thing.

"Would you like a glass of sherry?" he asked. I declined. After all his demonstrations of hospitality, he turned to the matter at hand, steepled his fingers, and laid it out for me with a direct statement. "I'm a federal auditor."

I tried not to register surprise. "Federal, as in IRS?"

"Federal, as in FBI," he answered and knew he had my interest. "Ever hear of the RICO Act?" he asked me. I nodded. I'd rather sit and look stupid than open my mouth and prove it. He undid his fingers in preparation of an explanation.

"RICO pertains mostly to organized crime and the Bureau has informants deep undercover in all the families," he said. "But I've been given some latitude with my investigation into a curious group of investors in commercial real estate here in Boston. Shall I go on?"

"Please do."

"The Bureau hasn't been known for its creativity, but J. Edgar Hoover's relatively recent demise has unleashed the floodgates of frustrated lawmen and jurists. Intrigued?"

This guy had sized me up in the smoker's lounge, played me, fooled me with his onyx ring and I enjoyed every turn and bump of the ride now. I respected a good cover. He took me for my change when I thought I was using his dime.

"May I call you Shane?"

"Sure."

"Level with me, Shane. Are you working for Brayton Braddock?"

I said nothing.

"I'll take your silence under advisement," he said and gave me an eloquent summation of the Racketeering Influenced and Corrupt Organizations Act. I'll admit I had assumed this special law pertained to guys with a lot of vowels in their names, to rackets such as interstate trucking, cigarette machines, bribery and white slavery, but Dunbar peaked my interest when he explained the finer shades of money laundering and real estate, and how auditing was like detective work.

"Ever hear of Jewish lightning?" he asked me.

"Can't say that I've heard the expression."

"A rather an unfortunate phrase," Dunbar said. "It's when the owner of building would rather pay an arsonist instead of spending money on repairs. Can you see how it falls under the auspices of RICO?"

Jimmy came to mind. Arson was lucrative business. I answered Dunbar.

"Conspiracy to commit insurance fraud, and then there's the opportunity to shift money around, or what you called money laundering. I'm sure there are cuter games to be played with real estate, too. Mind if I ask you a question?

"You wish to know if I'm investigating Brayton Braddock?"

"No, I assume you are. My question is, Why are you so forthcoming with me?"

"Why not? What can you do? Where can you go?" His hands lifted like the priest's did before he blessed the congregation. "You're an endangered species in this town, Shane Cleary. More than half of the police force wants you in the morgue. Now, I've heard a rumor that Braddock offered you a job. No need for you to admit as much, but I'd hate for you to get swept up in the net with him. Braddock might be an old friend, but he's trouble."

"I'd classify him as a childhood acquaintance and I'd leave it at that."

"Be that as it may, I lose nothing in my being candid with you, whether you work for the man or not." His hand moved. "This is one of several ledgers I've been reviewing. There is another one underneath it. Note the color of the first one." He closed it and showed me the spine. He put the two ledgers next to each for comparison. "Not your traditional shade of hunter green, are they?"

They weren't and he indicated a mark on the spine, imperceptible unless pointed out.

"This marked one is a master. The other one is a dummy."

"Two sets of books," I said. "And you just walked out of the Little Building with those?"

"There are several volumes," he said. "Nobody'll notice."

"I beg to differ." I rested, elbows on my thighs. "Need I remind you that Braddock and Company don't play nice, Mr. Dunbar? They might not get their hands dirty, but when they call in the job they don't leave any loose ends, and they wouldn't care less whether you're a government man or not. Doing what you're doing will get you the nap. Why bring the ledgers home? Why not continue using the Xerox machine?"

"Xerox?"

We both heard the creak of the front door opening. We looked at each other. I put my finger to my lips. I would go and check the door.

***

81

I don't remember much else. I had been hit. I had been hit hard, hard enough to lose consciousness.

There was the tunnel to the door and the white light, a voice, some coldness, and the Simon & Garfunkel lyric about darkness and silence in my head. I came to on the rug, face down and body sprawled out like I had danced the Charleston in my sleep. My head hung heavy as a bowling ball. I found a gun, my own in my hand. I feared the worst.

My eyes confirmed the horrible discovery. Dunbar sat dead in his chair. His head tilted forward as if he were showing me where the bullet had pin-cushioned him. The fireplace sputtered the last of its flames.

The ledgers were gone.

I checked my .38. I swung the cylinder out. All but one of my Nyclad bullets sat cozy in their chambers asleep. I glanced at the dead Dunbar. "Same bullet that killed Kennedy?"

Murder was one thing but the murder of a federal agent, another. Some mug had stage-managed me and I had first billing on the wanted poster, with my name five-feet high and spelled correctly. Homicide would love to collar me for this one.

Cherry lights outside were doing a Jackson Pollock against the windows and drapes. Boston police. Before the cops could reach the rear exit, I booked for the servant's entrance. These places always had one and I was grateful for Irish quarters. I forgot the Declaration of Independence, the Bill of Rights, the whole lot of it because none of it mattered now. I was on the lam, with Boston's best eager to put a toe tag on me first and ask questions later.

Chapter 12: Party in Progress

With cops at Dunbar's, I needed to become invisible. Bray and Cat lived nearby, so I hoofed it there for a word with Bray about those ledgers.

When the butler answered the door, I could hear the sounds of a party in progress. I was cold, slick with sweat, and hot for words with the master of the house.

"I wish to speak with Mr. Braddock. Tell him it's Shane Cleary."

The manservant's face looked unmoved and unsympathetic. He told me to step inside and wait in the hallway, as if I were a dog, while he informed Brayton. I wasn't having any of it and I barged in hard enough that he pivoted to avoid me and my damp coat.

Into the depths of the house, the music grew louder. I witnessed the awful spectacle of the embalmed in the main room. My social betters moved with impeccable manners, the circulation of conversation ebbed and flowed with polite nods, sips from a drink in one hand and the intake and release of smoke from a cigarette holder in the other.

I worked my own rhythm of foot forward and shoulder turns as I moved deeper into the forest of people. I caught some hard stares. I said hello here and there until I recognized the nape of the neck and exposed shoulders in front of me. Her head moved enough for me to view Bray and an attractive brunette in a dress so tight it breathed with her. Bankers and stockbrokers, young and old, around her were gaga as unrepentant schoolboys around a Playboy centerfold.

I lowered my lips to Cat's ear and imitated Bogart. "Who's the dame?"

Cat eyes registered surprise. Her left hand touched my cheek and she kissed the one closest to her lips. I didn't care if Bray saw or not. She pressed against me. Her hand dropped down, out of sight.

"Answer the question," I said.

"She's Bray's latest flavor, and for more than a month." Her voice and her hand continued the conversation. "She's a mathematician at MIT and the boys are all worked up over a program she says can predict the Stock Market."

"And they believe her?"

"Does she look like she has resorted to intimidation?"

Bray stepped forward. Cat's hand squeezed me and then drifted away. The glass he was holding said he was drinking martinis. He took one sip, looked at his wife, and then he focused his attention on me. "This is an unexpected surprise. A drink?"

"Not thirsty," I lied.

The adrenaline, the run here and the idea of cops after me for Dunbar made my mouth dry. My heart rate had subsided some, though my blood chilled in this terrarium of snakes and spiders. The sense of unease didn't end there. Bray had given me Dunbar's name, told me which building I'd find the man in. He had painted a portrait of blackmail for me, and I couldn't help but think he fitted me for the frame now that Dunbar was dead.

"You look dreadful." Bray said it as if he were an intern in his sixteenth hour and I was his last patient. "We should get you warmed up. I insist."

A kid appeared at his side. Sixteen if that, and a hundred pounds soaking wet, if you weighed her tuxedo jacket, the white shirt with black studs in it, and all the starch in her cuffs and collar. She wasn't Lolita in a bowtie, just some student there for the night, hoping to score easy cash. She sold Bray's caterer the bill that she was eighteen and could serve grown-up drinks to a bunch of degenerates. A girlfriend, somewhere in the room on this shift with her, must've offered advice on the makeup to boost her assets and tips because she had underlined that advice.

"A whiskey for Mr. Cleary here. Make it a double."

"No thanks, Bray; and no, thank you, miss."

She lowered her chin, stepped back into the crowd and disappeared. A banker-type to my left, a Harvey Wallbanger in his hand, watched her depart. She was in for a long night, this girl. I sampled the Forbes List around me that swallowed her up. This type of wealth spent its days at board meetings protecting the money earned in the last century, while they managed other people's cash in the new one. The wives clipped coupons and drank carburetor coffee because they wanted to save a dime. I never understood these people. They were mean to those they considered less than them, and mean with their money. Mean as in cruel, mean as in cheap.

"We should talk," I said to Bray. "In private."

Brayton didn't care that ears were listening. "Nothing you can't say here."

"You would prefer I didn't."

"Is everything all right?" a voice, avuncular and ancient, asked. With those clothes and that hair, he thought of himself as a suave Regis Philbin. I thought Bob Barker, only creepier and more decrepit. I recognized the type from St. Wystan's. About the same age as Lindsey but with more barnacles and decadence, the kind who considered himself a mentor to young impressionable boys, the way Aristotle tutored Alexander the Great.

"We're fine, Mr. Whipple," Bray answered. Drink in one hand, Bray's other hand grabbed me. I shrugged it off. "Let's go to our room with the fireplace," he said. "Shall we?"

"Like two patients etherized upon a table," I said, to quote Eliot's *Prufrock*. I skimmed faces, searched for Cat as I moved through the room, and found her. Face pale and downcast, she stared at me, champagne flute near her lips, close enough to me that I could see the life and death of bubbles inside the glass.

Bray stopped for a guest. I continued onward.

I turned the doorknob and flicked the switch and waited for him inside *our* room. I saw Bray through the open door. He said something to his guest and excused himself. He walked in, closed the door behind him, and pressed his back against it. There was a soft click and the slightest metallic sound of the lock as it turned behind him.

"Let's make this quick. I have company," he said.

The nerve. Prince Spaghetti Wednesday Nights existed in the North End because of his tribe. On the way in, I saw the food. Men dined on quiches, meatballs, and smoked salmon from platters doing the Tilt-A-Whirl around the room. The ladies restricted themselves to shrimp cocktails because it kept the needle on the scale to the ounce. It was toothpicks for forks and a Valium for a nightcap for them.

"Do you have an update for me?" Bray asked as he walked toward me. He had no intention of lighting the fireplace. Bray cocked back his martini glass and shook it to unloosen the olive that defied him. "I don't see why you couldn't have called," he said.

"I'll get straight to the point," I said. "What color are your ledgers?"

He squinted, suspicious of my question. "Hunter green. Why?"

"Not ordinary green, but that specific shade of green? Funny how green is symbolic of abundance, of nature and renewal, and also, greed and jealousy."

"Teaching symbolism in literature at Boston Latin in your spare time?"

He placed his glass on the mantel. His turn, I suppose, since I had put the snifter of brandy there the night he'd called me on his urgent matter of blackmail. This was all a game to him, except there was no ump in a chair to declare Game, Set, Match, and shout out his name. He rested his forearm against the mantelpiece and affected a jaunty pose. My serve apparently.

"You keep two sets of books."

He grinned. "You've been hard at work, I see. It's not some grand clue, Shane. Keeping two different sets of books is an open secret in the business world, especially when you are a publicly traded corporation."

"But you and your friends aren't public yet." I stepped closer to him. "You have to create that company first before you start buying up the waterfront."

I amused him.

"Look at you, Shane Cleary. You think you understand finance. Two books are legal, like I said. I won't trouble you with talk about depreciation and expenses, projected or real." He lowered his arm and stuck a hand into a pocket in his jacket. Another pose. "Are we finished?" he said.

"You're right, I wouldn't understand the arcane vocabulary, but I do know common words such as 'fraud' and 'laundry'." He huffed derision. I was about to repeat a clip of what Dunbar said to me about the RICO Act when we both heard a soft knock on the door, and then the sound of a key turning the lock. These two had His and Her keys to the room.

"I believe this is the wife," I said.

"She probably noticed my absence."

"Or she's here to tell you the king shouldn't neglect the aristocracy."

The way he tilted his head suggested he was ready to respond with something clever, but whatever it might've been evaporated. Wit required intelligence; sarcasm didn't. Bray crossed the room, pulled Cat into the room and shut the door behind her.

She glanced at me, then at her husband in search of an explanation. I rather enjoyed my role as usurper to the social scene as she wondered what we had discussed.

"Is everything all right?" she asked.

The fright in her eyes vanished. She stood there in her von Furstenberg wrap. The silk jersey clung to terrain I knew well from our last encounter. She leveled a familiar stare at me and said, "Say something."

"I'm not qualified. Isn't that right, Bray?"

She turned to her husband, eyes keen on him. "What is he referring to?"

"Doesn't concern you," Bray said.

"Don't you dare condescend to speak to me with that tone."

"I wasn't patronizing you," Bray said to her and, when he sensed I was leaving, asked me, "Where are you going?"

"I'm done here."

Brayton rushed to block the door, panic in his voice. "Any word about blackmail?"

I glared at him. Cat eased up beside him, eyes sad. I could guess what she was thinking. "I should go," I said. He demanded that I'd stay. I wouldn't.

"Let's get something straight, here and now, Bray. I work for a living, unlike some people. I'm not your pet." I bowed my head to her. "I'll call next time. Good night."

I closed the door behind me, softly and with delicacy. Not smug, but I was smiling. I asked one of the hired staff where I might find the washroom, and she provided me with two possibilities. I don't know why I said washroom.

Bathroom was a perfectly acceptable word.

The restroom on the ground floor was occupied, so I climbed the stairs to the second one. There was no need for me to knock. The door opened and then slammed shut. The light inside stuttered like a flash of lightning. Voices. A man and woman arguing. She tried to escape the room and him. The door opened and closed again. I'd seen a flash of white shirt before the door slammed shut a third time. I seized the doorknob and worked my shoulder into the wood.

Terrified and trapped in a small pace with Harvey Wallbanger, the server girl I had seen earlier was on the vanity, knees pulled against her, topless. I whipped a hand towel from a ring on the wall and snapped it in his face. His hands flew up to his eyes. I slammed him against the wall and kneed him. I yanked him up and shoved the terrycloth towel into his open hole.

"You've done enough," I said and stared into his frightened, bloodshot eyes. He whimpered around the plug in his mouth. His hands cupped his injured parts. I rubbed my fingers together like a cricket worked his wings for a song. "Your wallet, please." When he resisted, I grabbed a handful of hair and pulled his head back. His eyes widened in disbelief. "I said, your wallet."

His hand trembled and touched his breast. I flipped his lapel over as if I had touched garbage. I teased out what money he carried and tossed his Brooks Brothers billfold on the floor. I turned to the girl on the counter.

Mascara streaked, breath uneven, she was off the counter, tux shirt on and facing the mirror, trying to make herself decent. The bowtie gone, her hands shook as she worked the studs back into her shirt.

"You okay?" I asked. Stupid question.

She shook her head. She devoted herself to her task, until a stud fell to the floor and she cursed and started crying.

"Forget it," I said. "Here, take this, and find your jacket." I handed her the folded bills. "Go home," I said and reached into my pocket for change and gave it to her. "Call yourself a cab."

I told her where she could find the nearest payphone. She didn't thank me. She didn't say a word. She looked at her attacker. Her jaw moved and then tensed. For a second there, I thought she would spit in his face. She squeezed her eyes shut and then opened them instead. She touched the side of my arm, and left.

***

After I threw Harvey out and did my business, I went back downstairs. I adjusted the sleeves of my coat when I heard Sinatra in the main room. I recognized the tune. Frank Sinatra after Ava Gardner, Sinatra with Nelson Riddle. Loving and leaving, Sinatra learned from Ava how to sing a torch song with feeling, with authenticity. After her, he wore a suit of armor. Forever more. Nobody would hurt him like she had. I thought about that, about Frank, about Cat and me, and the fedora in Jimmy's shop.

I peeked into the room on my way out. "I Love You" banged on, and I remembered the first time I had heard the song was in the film *Stalag 17*. My eyes were ready to quit the room, tired of the crowd I'd swum through earlier, until I spotted Cat in the swell, alone and lonely as an inmate. While Frank wrung those notes, Cat watched her husband dance with the tasty brunette. I knew that look, angry and offended enough that it could devein shrimp.

Chapter 13: Person of Interest

I needed dark streets and time to think, time and distance away from Beacon Hill. I wandered two miles into Cambridge, into a pool hall and bar in Central Square in need of a payphone. I wouldn't chance using any of the call boxes on Mass Ave because addicts used them to call their dealers and arrange for drops. Central Square had three things going for it: a Chinese restaurant, Ken's Steakhouse, and a movie house named after Orson Welles. What worked against it, in no descending order, were all the drugs, the deals, the sexual assaults, and the Cantab Lounge, which rivaled the Blood and Bucket in my South End for the raucous and ridiculous. The Square made me think of Bray because a few years ago this neighborhood blocked developers and politicians who asserted eminent domain to level buildings and lay down a highway through the middle of Central Square.

My nerves wavered between fever and exhaustion, first with Dunbar and then Bray and Cat. The girl in the bathroom had spiked my temperature. I stepped inside the establishment.

The only white things in the place were the lights and cue balls on a billiard table. I moved through intentional darkness towards the payphone on the far wall. I untangled the rat's tail of a cord first, and tried my luck with the coin return. Empty. My hand dove into my pocket for a dime. I dialed Lindsey's number. I did all that under the scrutiny of a black man near me.

My eyes read the room. I was the novelty item in this toy store and none of the children looked happy. "Professor?"

I hear Lindsey pull the chain to his nightlight.

"You have any idea what time it is?"

"Don't care," I said. "Look, I'm jammed up and I need your help."

Someone pointed at me and shared a laugh with his buddy next to him. The contrast between the professor's domesticity in my ear and my urban plight before my eyes were not lost on me. I spoke while an audience formed a line to watch me use the phone.

I summarized my visit to the Little Building, my talk with Security, and included the exclusive smoker's lounge on the mezzanine floor. "I found and talked to the accountant," I said.

"The guy Bray thought was blackmailing him?"

"He was an auditor."

"Was?" The professor had the copy-editor's ear for the past tense.

"Was, and now there are boys in blue looking for me."

My audience had lost interest, except for one guy.

"Dunbar is dead. This isn't making any sense, Shane."

The exception with an interest in me was a Joe Frazier look-alike. He approached the bar with a pool stick that could pass for a piece of chalk in his hand. I watched him and the barkeep talk, eyes over at me between sentences.

"I need you to do something for me," I said to Lindsey.

"Anything. What?"

"Go to my office pronto. You have a key. Get Delilah the hell out of there. Bring her to your place. Her carrier is in the closet on the right when you come in the door."

I knew flatfeet and detectives and how much they respected me. They wouldn't think twice about putting Delilah on Death Row at a kill shelter. I gave Lindsey the number for Security at the Little Building. I told him to tell the man I would call in the morning, and that he should expect Homicide detectives to ask questions about Dunbar. Security might not have not logged the name Fletcher in, as a favor for my past good deed, but something told me the police inked me in the log book for Dunbar's murder. A person of interest.

Boston's finest would act fast before the Feds showed up. They would attack my office and my apartment. I was okay with the apartment. The

91

uniforms would have their hands full with my landlord screaming at them about overdue rent while they turned the place upside down. My office was in a commercial building. The other tenants with serious money would start calling other important people if the police disrupted business.

Lindsey asked about the Xerox machine, and I told him that I hadn't had time. He reminded me: "It's on the third floor."

"There's no third floor."

"What? I worked there for three whole weeks, my longest assignment. There's a third floor."

Lindsey used the same voice when he expressed frustration with the job hunt, how nobody would hire someone his age. I heard complaint and rebuttal like they were a call and response in a blues song. He was somebody, he'd tell me. He possessed a rich and diverse range of experience, a multitude of talents. Whitman had multitudes, too, enough so that the poet resorted to self-publishing *Leaves of Grass* because nobody cared about poetry. Lindsey would ramble about his qualifications. He was responsible, he'd say, and knew how to spell the word, too. He was someone, he'd repeat again and again.

I kept eyes on Frazier. A friend joined him while Lindsey ranted on about the third floor.

"It doesn't matter," I told him

"Clearly," I heard next, sarcasm attached.

"Please do what I asked."

I might've said a word or two about kibble and treats. I don't remember because I prioritized personal safety next. Half of a ton of conversation headed my way. I wanted to tell Lindsey about the money under my floorboard, that he should take it and fly south to Florida for the winter if he didn't hear from me in three days, but I didn't. I hung up. I had two visitors.

"Gentlemen," I said.

"John don't like no dealers or cops, and he don't like weapons on the premises."

"I'm no dealer, and I'm no cop. I came in to use the phone." I said it with politeness and I included the bartender with a look during my exchange with his two messengers.

Frazier responded, "If you're ain't either, then why're you packing?"

"Guys, I needed the phone and I've used it, so I'll be on my way now."

Frazier's buddy crossed his thick arms. The room turned silent. Morgues had more noise. I was ecstatic the stand-in for the boxer had set aside his pool stick. I went to move and Frazier blocked me. I stepped back, exposed both hands. I sized the two men up.

A boxer worked the body. Ribs are softer than a head. Nothing made a human being panic faster than losing his relationship with oxygen. An opponent short on air in his lungs dropped his arms. I counted three tires of blubber around Frazier's friend's midsection. Frazier himself had no neck and telephone poles for arms. He was wide, tall and darker in mood.

"Fellows," the bartender yelled. The two heads in front of me corkscrewed right and listened. John the barkeep and owner spoke: "Sit your asses on down or get back to your game of pool. Leave the man alone, and don't make me say it twice."

The patter of conversation in the hall resumed. I heard an order to rack'em and soon there was the loud crack of billiard balls. I wandered over to the bar.

Tight Afro and Richard Roundtree muttonchops, John leveled very clear eyes at me. I could count the pulses in his brachial and carotid arteries. A baritone voice spoke to me.

"You don't belong in here. You're carrying on my property, and I don't like it. I'd suggest you turn tail while you still have feathers."

"I needed a phone. I had a problem."

"You used it, and we all have problems."

I showed my hands again. I reached into my pocket for money. I placed a Grant on the counter between us. He glanced at it and then at me. "May I sit?" I asked.

"Always been a free country for you."

The two pillars of the community reappeared and sandwiched me. They weren't there to order drinks. "Is this fool here a friend of yours, John?"

"For the moment, and now screw off, the both of ya."

I flashed a smile to each of my two bookends. When I faced John again, the fifty-dollar bill was gone and a short glass appeared in its wake. John had one elbow on the counter, while his other hand held a bottle. Johnny Walker Black Label. He poured me a double.

"Enjoy your drink, and then walk your problems on out the door."

There was a ruckus behind us and John lifted his head up like an exam proctor. The sounds withered into silence. I sipped a taste of the scotch.

"You said everyone has problems. What are yours?" I asked.

"You my shrink, or what? Is this you trying to establish rapport?"

"Making conversation is all." I watched his hand move. He picked up a dish towel.

"I'm not your friend." John's eyes narrowed. "I've got problems, you excluded. Problem one is this town. Problem two is over two hundred years old."

I toasted him. "Mine started this evening."

That tickled him. "You are something." John turned over a short glass. He poured himself some Walker. "You say you're no dealer or a cop, but you're carrying. You're not one of them Winter Hill boys, are you?"

"No," I answered. "Why, do you think all of us Irish look alike?" My joke fell flat, so I played honest. "I do my best to avoid them. And cops."

Either he nodded in agreement, or Johnny Walker pleased his throat.

"Have a problem with Winter Hill boys?" I asked.

"Who doesn't?"

It wasn't hard math. The crew from Somerville demanded protection money, like the Italians in the North End did. Pay, or deliveries fell off the truck. Pay up or your drivers experienced migraines from a baseball bat to the head or some other form of mischief. John, like most businessmen, probably accepted the tax as part of the cost of doing business. What probably bothered him, what annoyed him, was how minority business owners like him paid twice into the protection racket. Irish and Italian.

"The way you talk…," I said and paused. "You're not from around here, are you?"

"Like a dog after a bone with that rapport, aren't you?"

"Suit yourself. Trying to make conversation," I said. "I'll move on to my next problem."

"And what problem is that, exactly?" John asked.

"Finding a place for the night."

My answer perplexed John.

"You don't look homeless."

"I'm not," I said.

"Your problem then?" John asked.

"The authorities are laying siege to my home and livelihood. No concern of yours."

John had taken to cleaning a glass with a towel. "All by your lonesome with iron in your back pocket," he said. "All kinds of authorities in this town."

Relaxed from drink, consoled that Delilah was safe with Lindsey, and that the professor would have word out to Security in the Little Building, I said, "Thanks for the drink. You didn't answer where you're from. Never mind, it doesn't matter."

The highball glass John was cleaning shone bright. The sparkle would make Madge from Palmolive envious. I stood up, adjusted the bar stool, and prepared to leave. I told him I'd tell him something that he probably already knew, but I'd say it anyway.

"You said problem number one was this town, this home of patriots, and the cradle of liberty, for everyone except you, despite the fact that Crispus Attucks, a black man, was the first to die in the rich man's Revolution, and we all know how that all worked out for your people. He's buried in a small graveyard on Tremont Street."

John's eyes glistened and the pulse in his neck quickened.

"And your view on my problem number two?" he asked me.

"Two hundred years old and counting? Look at your hands, John. Go on, look at them."

John opened up his hands and considered them.

"No matter how many times you wash them, they won't go white."

John pointed to the vacated barstool. "Sit down, and tell me what you could possibly know about a black man's problem."

"I can't, but I can empathize and relate."

"Oh, you're one of those cotton liberals, all fluffy and white, and—"

I put out my hand. "Name is Shane Cleary. I'm Irish. I was a cop. I'm still Irish."

John extended his hand, slowly and with caution. We shook. Johnny Walker was there on the bar. I glanced at the bottle. He nodded, so I poured myself a finger.

Without too many details, I explained how I testified against a fellow police officer who had shot an unarmed black kid, a child no more than fourteen years old, going about his business in a tenement building, and by business, I meant coming home after a game of basketball in a lot filled with broken bottles, and home to hallways with roaches and rats. I mentioned another black boy named Pratt, murdered in similar circumstances, and how a year later a white woman named Evelyn Wagler had been set on fire on Blue Hill Avenue in Dorchester.

"I know my history, Mr. Cleary. I know how the Irish were treated in Boston."

"Poor people have poverty and police in common."

"But some of you Irish became cops, and part of the problem. Explain that to me, Mr. Cleary."

"Speaking for myself, I ran wild as a kid and it was a cop who cut me a break. I've tried to pay the kindness back."

"Your folks?" John asked.

"Mom died from a broken heart after my father blew his brains out. He wasn't a cop."

"I'm sorry to hear that." John raised his glass.

"And you?" I asked.

"From Chicago, South Side, by way of Mississippi."

"Whereabouts in Mississippi?" I asked.

"Place so poor, we couldn't afford a word for dirt." John knocked back the last of his Walker. He refreshed my glass. "The boy killed in the housing project," he said. "I didn't realize you were the one who stood up for him in court. I suppose you'd like a thank you note on behalf of the black community?"

"No, but a place for the night would be nice."

John took out my fifty-dollar bill and placed it on the bar. "Keep it, and give me a minute to call my old lady."

Chapter 14: No Hemingway

I spotted the unmarked car on Boylston Street, a green Plymouth Fury, in front of the Little Building. Surveillance mistake number one: the car sat so heavy on the mark it didn't let the place breathe. Mistake number two—and I blame the car depot clerk for this one—the vehicle's visit to the car wash in the middle of December stripped the car of any spontaneity. Then there was mistake number three: the two sailors in the front seat didn't match the boat. The coffee cup on the dashboard was from a known hangout for cops in Revere Beach.

The little hand on the Timex on my wrist ticked towards ten. I pulled Security's card out. He was on today. I hoped his phone wasn't tapped. I doubted bug men worked that fast, but you never knew. Security seemed like the kind of guy who caught on quick. Black folks in this town are either born with second sight or develop it fast.

There was one last thing that bothered me. There was no patrolman in the intersection directing traffic. I dropped my dime. I would know within seconds from Security's voice if there was artillery inside the building. I punched the number to the Front Desk. I left loose change on top of the box. I intended the first call as a hang-up. Security might latch on that the second call was yours truly.

"Good morn—" he said and I hung up.

That confirmed he was on deck. I had an eye on that Plymouth and for anything and everything that walked up to it or around it. So far, the Hardy Boys were in neutral. It was painful for me to watch them, even if I wasn't a cop. The driver might as well have had lipstick on the rim of his coffee cup.

I placed the second call.

"Good morning, Little Building."

"It's me. Say something to keep this conversation alive."

"No, sir, Mr. Sullivan."

"Got company in the lobby?"

"Yes, sir. Two packages, but you'll have to sign for them at the front desk. I apologize for the inconvenience but policy is policy, unless the deliveries are made at the freight elevators downstairs. Signatures aren't needed there. What's that?"

He was good. He just told me where to expect company and where I might not expect any hassles. I asked him, "Is the freight elevator near the subway entrance? Any cops there?" I wanted to bite my tongue. I had asked him two questions.

"Yes, sir." He paused a natural beat. "No, sir. Will that be all—oh, wait. I almost forgot to mention your secretary forgot her pass this morning, so I issued her a temporary one. You ought to talk to her. Which secretary? Right, you have several girls reporting to you. The new girl. She had *Anna Karenina* on her this morning." He allowed another beat for the ocean wave to leave sand in my mouth. He ended with, "You, too. You have a nice day, Mr. Sullivan."

The click about devastated me, but not so much as what I saw across from me. I recognized the caveman's gait, the strongman's disproportionate upper body to puny legs. He had a bucket hat on his head like the famous cop Frank Serpico, but that was about where the comparison ended. Shades hid the eyes. The bastard turned his head to the Plymouth and I could swear that the cop on the passenger side lifted a hand to indicate the Little Building.

The walk belonged to the Boston Barbarian, a notorious hit man and veteran of the War Between the Hibernians, the feud between the McLaughlin Mob and the Winter Hill Gang. A protracted purge was bad for business and the mafia wanted to work with a winner, so the Italians sent the Barbarian in to expedite the carnage. Forty bodies filled up the morgue, in '67 alone.

The Barbarian made Bugsy Siegel and Albert Anastasia look like demure schoolgirls. The only trait he shared with those two mobsters was that he took sadistic delight in his job. The Irish feared him. The Italians loathed him. His own lawyers despised him. A credible source I knew within the Bureau put it in my ear the Barbarian was an informant. His handler had gone native. Massachusetts and Rhode Island had no shortage of bodies and last I heard from my Bureau buddy was that the Barbarian had been sent out west for a vacation for all the unwanted attention.

The Little Building was on his itinerary. The Barbarian headed for the front door. I wanted to be disgusted with a lot of things, but I had a problem: the professor was inside and, if Tolstoy was any indication of Russian authors I've read, this story didn't promise a happy ending.

I scanned the street for the subway stop and UPS truck. I found the truck halfway up the block, in all its Pullman-brown glory, but no sign of a cap or uniform anywhere.

I crossed Boylston behind the Plymouth. I spotted the deliveryman. He was whistling his way up the inclined street from the Transportation Building with his hand truck. He had eyes on his clipboard. A ring of keys dangled on his left hip and a clip-on set of cards bounced on his right. I knew what I had to do, but I was rusty at the pickpocket gig.

I did the bump and "Excuse me," and patted the guy with the "I'm so sorry" with one hand while my other hand reached in and unclipped the prize. I moved quickly to the door's box and swiped any old card until I heard the latch lift and pulled the door. "Thank you, IBM," I said to myself. I ran down a long empty tunnel in the direction of the Little Building.

The Otis lift was a metal-grated cube that resembled a floating jail cell. I slid the grate and looked for the captain's helm. I'll be damned: the professor had been right.

There was a third floor.

Call it an angels flight, a man-lift, or dumbwaiter, but it took serious driving skills to move a mousetrap this size a 150-feet per minute and park it level to the floor of its destination. Dial set to 3, I drove granny-style, nice and slow, eyes forward on the wall for the floor numbers.

¡Uno...dos...tres!

I had no idea what awaited me on the other side of the accordion metal.

The large room was horror-movie quiet. I heard a mechanical sound. I padded softly. I eased my .38 out of its holster. The back of my neck tingled. I located the noise. The copier machine spat out a piece of paper.

"Hands up where I can see them."

"Don't shoot."

The professor popped up like a target on the shooting range in *Magnum Force* and I was Dirty Harry Callahan, ready to decide between bogey or law-abiding citizen, blast the bad guy and spare the civilian.

No sooner I lowered my piece, than a door flung up. The Barbarian.

"Down!" I screamed and crouched low. There were no shots. Yet.

The Barbarian took cover behind a column. The professor crawled around the copier, stuck his hand up to the glass to grab whatever it was that he had been copying before I interrupted him. His movement earned a round into the Xerox.

"I told you there was a third floor," he said.

I pointed to the elevator. "Move when I tell you and stay low." He hugged two ledgers and Tolstoy to his chest. "Now," I said.

The professor bolted and I rolled across the floor, eyes and finger aiming for a shinbone, a drumstick of a leg, or anything attached to the Barbarian.

I fired.

I heard a profanity about my mother. I heard a thud, and back-pedaled my retreat.

I was a foot away, back to the elevator with the professor inside, when the Barbarian charged us, shooting as he advanced. I hadn't had that many bullets zing past my ears since Vietnam. It's something you never forgot. The hair inside your ears heats up and a crazy warmth melts inside your head.

I fired back.

He had a forward's speed. I thought this guy couldn't be that lousy of a shot, and then it hit me. I wasn't his primary target.

The professor yanked me into the cage, and slammed the grate closed. He threw himself against the side wall. Incoming fire sparked off the grates. Crazy bastard. I jammed the captain's needle downward-ho.

I eased back on the helm to soften our landing, then threw the metal curtain

101

open. The professor and I darted for the door and Boylston Street. As we crossed the street, I looked downwind and saw my two friends in the Fury gas it into the Little Building. Shots fired. The professor and I were halfway across the Common when we stopped running. Adrenaline had made a runner of Lindsey, with the ledgers and Tolstoy still crushed to his chest. My lungs burned. I was winded and I worried I'd throw up. I was glad I'd quit smoking after the Douglas trial.

"What the hell were you thinking?" I asked, once I caught my breath.

"I was trying to help, and—" He gasped and raised his hand for mercy.

I waited until his panting subsided. "And what?"

"I'd told you there was a third floor."

"Unbelievable. You win, Professor. There's a third floor. Let me see those."

I relieved him of the ledgers and novel. I examined the ledgers. The mark was there on the spine, but I was more interested in the Tolstoy. That he kept Count Leo between his heart and the ledgers was a good thing. The Barbarian had cleared a round through one of the thick ledgers. I found the slug inside *Anna K*. I laughed the madman's laugh and hugged the professor. He didn't understand until he saw it. He, too, was thankful that Tolstoy had been no Hemingway with words.

Chapter 15: Soul Food

"Delilah is fine. Tell me more about this Barbarian character."

We were sitting in the back room of Sister Sylvia's, a restaurant in Dorchester. Sylvia was both the cook and owner of the eatery and she had given me room and board there because John had asked her to. Delano Lindsey tried not to eat like a heathen but failed. Our encounter with a notorious killer had boosted his appetite.

He was buttering a biscuit and didn't look at me while he ate. I had my fork up to the tines in Sylvia's signature dish of chicken and waffles. She had topped off a succulent portion of the bird, which she battered and fried in a proprietary blend of salt and spices, with her secret maple-bourbon syrup. A napkin on my lap, I had coffee and orange juice within reach.

"Is she eating?" I asked him.

"Since when have you known a cat not to eat?"

"Good appetite?"

"Delilah is fine, Shane. In fact, she slept next to me last night. I asked you about the Barbarian, so please stop being evasive."

That hurt. I was jealous. Here I was on the run, lodged in a small garret above a woman's kitchen, tormented to sleep by the smell of slow-cooked ribs and waking up to the aroma of bread baking, and my cat had two-timed me.

"Slept with you, huh? She was probably cold and needed body warmth."

I was mad at him for going to the Little Building, but grateful we'd survived and that we had a ledger. We'd eluded the Barbarian and two cops.

Dunbar said there were more ledgers and I had evidence of the two-ledger system in my possession. Legal or not, it could cast a shadow on Brayton, if the right pair of eyes examined them for irregularities. Meanwhile the professor dipped his biscuit into white-sausage gravy. I reminded him he shouldn't have been there. "I didn't ask you to play Spenser."

"Thought you preferred Marlowe."

"And I'd prefer you boys shut up and eat," cut in a voice from behind the curtain of beads in the doorway. We both stood up for the lady. "I give you boys my private dining room and all you do is bicker on like two married crows." She realized we were standing. "Do I look like Mother Superior to you? Sit your asses down."

Sylvia was John's wife. She pulled up a chair and joined us. She was a small-boned woman with a voice like Ma Rainey who cooked like a chef with a Michelin star for southern cuisine. She and John made the oddest of couples. He was tall and massive, a man who chewed chicken bones for fun. This petite lady ruled him. Her presence compelled courtesies, such as 'Yes, ma'am' and 'No, ma'am.'

"How is my food?"

"Delicious," I said.

"Delectable," the professor said.

"That's what I like to hear. Now, here's the thing you both need to hear and understand. It might not be right my overhearing your conversation, but I did hear the name Barbarian. I'd never seen the man with my own eyes, but any fool who's lived in this town knows the man is a killer, so I want to say, here and now in unequivocal terms, Mr. Shane, that if you have any ideas about involving my John in whatever business you've got with the Barbarian, then I'd suggest you put it out of your head."

"I can speak for myself, Syl," John said.

The beads swung right and settled back into a veil behind him.

"I'm just looking out for you, baby," she said.

"I can do that all by myself, thank you." He squeezed her from behind with his broad hands and kissed her on the cheek. The professor and I looked down at our food.

"I don't like crazy white folks, John." She looked to us. "I don't mean you

104

boys. I was talking about the Barbarian and his kind. We clear?"

"Yes, ma'am."

John asked for a dish of her chicken and waffles, saying please

Sylvia put her smallish hand on her man's chest and then walked away. John pulled his chair back to make room for his legs. "You had a run-in with the Barbarian?"

"More like he ran at us," I said. The professor added 'shooting at us' a second later. He wasted no time sopping up the last of the tasty gravy. John looked incredulous at the man's appreciation for soul food. The professor asked John if Sylvia would pan-fry another biscuit for him. "Go on, and ask her yourself. She don't bite," John answered.

"He eats when he's nervous," I said.

"I do not."

"I forgot. You read the rest of the time."

John scratched an ear. "And what's your take on this situation with the Barbarian? I ask because I don't want that man bothering my woman or my bar. She's worked hard to build up this restaurant. I won't forgive myself should something happen to her, or this place."

The professor didn't miss the moment. "His business is with Shane. Your wife is of no concern to the Barbarian."

John put both elbows on the table. He said what I was thinking. "You do read too much."

"What's that supposed to mean?" Lindsey said. "I'll have you two know I don't live in some fantasy world. I know what's out there."

I was done with my meal. I placed my napkin next to the dish. I took in a deep breath before I spoke. "No, you don't, Professor. The Barbarian is a walking nightmare. John is right. The longer I stay here, the more likely it is that the Barbarian will show up. I've imposed on John and Sylvia's hospitality long enough."

"Is the Barbarian that bad?" Lindsey asked. "Yes, he's a gangster, but it's my understanding there are rules."

John seesawed from one elbow to another. His head craned forward for emphasis on what he wanted to say to Delano Lindsey, formerly of St.

Wystan's and Harvard University. "This ain't *The Godfather*. His business is murder. Pure and simple." To me he asked, "What's his argument with you, Mr. Cleary?"

"Don't quite know yet."

"Know who hired him out?"

"Take your pick," I said. "Someone dirty at City Hall, someone within the BPD. Hell, cops in front of the building let him walk right in."

"Payback for Douglas?"

"A bit delayed and extreme, but could be."

"Any chance it's your client?"

The professor interrupted. "They do have history."

John wanted details, like a banker did before he approved a loan. I had to be honest.

"Let's say it's personal."

"How personal is this history between you?"

"I slept with his wife."

The professor added more commentary. "But that's all in the past," and glanced over at me for confirmation, but I looked away.

Sylvia appeared with a platter of food for John in one hand and a dispenser of ordinary maple syrup in the other. We shut up and let her serve her husband. She bused our dishes. Her stern look my way reminded me of our conversation about John. Other than that, she was all smiles and good cheer. The professor sought an extra biscuit from her. When we heard the shiver of the beads, we knew she was on her way to the kitchen and we could resume our conversation. John asked me for a description of the Barbarian. I gave him the quick sketch of ugly and mean.

"I think I've met the man," John said. He related the shakedown at his bar for us. "Handed him two-grand. I don't think he was collecting for his North End friends, or his Irish buddies in the Winter Hill crowd, because he came alone. He told me to count on inflation next month. Looks like and sounds like he's freelancing to me."

"He can do that?" the professor asked.

"He could and he did," John said.

"Remember Mayor Curley?" I asked the professor. When he nodded, I retold the story for John's benefit, of the time the mayor and future governor—who had been elected alderman while in prison for mail fraud—needed a loan. A certain gangster loaned Curley the money with the politician's life as insurance. This story, I told John, might be apocryphal. The ward politics, corruption, and jail time were not, and neither was the next story about the Barbarian.

Once, the Barbarian had received the blessing to take out another gangster. Protocol in the underworld was that a friend of the victim did the job. The mob didn't like it when civilians got gummed up in the wet works, nor did they tolerate creative thinking. A simple gunshot to the head sufficed. I could tell the professor didn't like my slow pace. "Get to the point," he said.

"The Barbarian knew the mark and his whole family. Rather than shoot the guy he set fire to the man's building and waited for him to exit. The problem was that the guy's mother and relatives lived in that building." I let that hang in the air.

"And?" the professor asked.

"He shot all of them as they fled the building. He considered it target practice."

"And the mob let him get away with that?"

John answered. "Man's still among the living, ain't he?" John worked his knife and fork through the meat and waffles, despite the unsavory conversation.

The beads swayed in an unexpected breeze. None of us liked the odds, but the Barbarian was a variable in the equation with Braddock and his stable of bluebloods. The BPD was another matter, especially after my confrontation in Bay Village and Dunbar's death. I needed a favor from John.

"Drive the professor home for me," I told him. "The professor is done with adventures. If he tries anything stupid, you tell Sylvia to take care of him. Can she do that?"

John rotated in his seat to warn Lindsey. "She'll feed you like it was Thanksgiving Day, but move one wrong inch and she'll spatchcock you like you was yesterday's chicken."

Sylvia entered the room with the urgency of a Western Union telegram burning her hand. She thrusted the newspaper in front of me. I read the headline.

MAN FOUND MURDERED IN FENS

My eyes dropped into the column for details. The Fens was Jimmy's neck of the woods, a patch of marshland and mosquitoes, a lot of mud, and an area notorious for homosexuals in the bushes at night. *Roger Sherman dead* was the first blow. Reading *a concerned citizen has come forward with information, but his name is being withheld to ensure his safety* was the second.

All good things came in threes. *Shane Cleary is a person of interest in the deaths of businessman Roger Sherman and Nathaniel Dunbar, a federal auditor. Mr. Cleary is a private investigator…* I folded the paper and sipped warm OJ. The newspaper skimped on accuracy: 'federal' could mean a lot of little things. I had assumed Dunbar was IRS. My guess on the omission was that the BPD bought time before they notified the FBI. Local and federal law enforcement got on together the way orange juice tasted after you brushed your teeth.

"You look paler than Casper the Friendly Ghost," John said. Sylvia tried to take the paper but John intercepted it. "We should go, Lindsey," he said and rose from his chair.

"What about my biscuit?"

"Take it with you."

An idea washed over me. "Ever been to a gay bar, John?"

"A sissy bar? Uh, can't say I have, but there's a first time for everything."

Sylvia stood there, her face full of questions she didn't dare ask. Her forehead creased with worry for John and her face hardened into a mask for me. "You're responsible for him," she said and pointed a finger at me. "You bring him back, you hear. The Barbarian will be the least of your worries if you don't."

"Yes, ma'am."

A cop had beaten me. The Barbarian had taken a shot at me. The Boston Police hated me enough that they didn't need an excuse to crush me like a cigarette butt on the sidewalk. Brayton Braddock disliked me. A cat was angry with me. A woman haunted me. Now, Boston journalists were one keystroke away from writing my obituary.

Chapter 16: Saying No to the Devil

I drove John's car. He read his newspaper. The chauffeur routine was cute enough to draw stares from black kids playing stickball between the spurts of traffic on their street. A white man driving a black man was a sight they had never seen in their young lives. The pages of the newspaper rustled like a moth trapped in cellophane.

"Says here Roger Sherman was found with a bullet to the back of the head. Sounds professional. Think it's the Barbarian?"

"Doesn't add up right for me. What's the connection between the Barbarian and Sherman?"

"Like you expected his ass at the Little Building."

At the light, I worked a diagram of a fish out for John. I started from the tail, with the Missing Persons assignment from Bill, and worked my way to Roger Sherman at the head of my fish. Each fact along the way was a detail, a bone. Jimmy and our conversation. A bone. I visited Bay Village. Another bone. I found what I found there and received the reception I received. Bone. Jimmy again, and that last one stuck in the throat: Marty Savitz, his office and his wall of athletes. I hashed it all out while John consumed the paper.

"So, the late Roger Sherman was into blackmail and the sex trade," John said after he reached over and placed the paper on the leather next to me. "That much would be clear to Helen Keller. I've heard of Jimmy C. Who hasn't? Question is whether he killed Roger. You said him and Roger were friends, so maybe Roger was blackmailing him, too."

"Doubt it," I said. "They were more than just friends."

"Business partners in the sex trade?"

"Perhaps. Perhaps not," I said, with a cut of the wheel onto the ramp for 93-South into Boston. "If Jimmy was being blackmailed or he was involved in it, then he would've wanted the roll of film I found, or he'd at least check the camera, knowing that it was there."

"Maybe he knew you got to it before he had the chance."

"Jimmy wouldn't have had any qualms about searching me for it, but he didn't."

"You had a gun."

"Across the room when he showed up. And don't forget he held a cleaver to a cop's throat. Jimmy told me the sex club was Roger's thing."

"And you believe a man with a cleaver?"

"I believe a man that could've used it on me, but didn't. That's what I believe."

"You're saying Jimmy suddenly remembered this meeting with Marty, came and saved your ass from the po-lice."

The accent on the first syllable was sarcasm for my benefit. I looked. He smiled.

I asked John, "Ever stop to think the cop was being blackmailed, or that he was in on the party scene?"

"Shit, what I think is you don't want to entertain the idea Bill and his buddies might've set you up. He's a cop. Where's his loyalty at? Maybe you fixate on hockey and Savitz because it's easier not to think your friend Bill might've stayed behind that big ol' blue line. Amirite?" John included a Colgate smile with his question.

I gripped the steering wheel hard.

John continued his theory. "Ain't this the Macy's Thanksgiving Day parade? We haven't even talked about the dead turkey in the room that's got the police lined to do a body cavity search on you. Let's talk Beacon Hill. We don't know whether someone saw you or not at Dunbar's, but ain't it your good luck to have the police show up? Maybe, Bill—"

"Bill would never do that," I said.

"And why not? Oh, that's right. The two of you were soul brothers in the Army. I can dig that. Point man, you said." John whistled through his teeth.

111

"Sounds to me like he's pointed at you."

"Bill is different."

"Hooah. Army battle cry, right? You two were mud fuckers way back in the day on the other side of the world, but life has changed since then in these United States. You keep on filleting your fish, Mr. Cleary. I hate to break it to you, but you're not in the Army and you're no longer part of the Fraternal Order of Police. This a different jungle right here, in Beantown, USA. Give me one good reason why Bill couldn't have done it. One good excuse why the shoes don't fit your boy?"

I let some seconds pass between us. I saw the skyline, the silent girders of new construction rising up. Cobb, the architect, proposed blue glass. Others had suggested a séance to summon Puritan judges to burn him at the stake in front of Trinity Church for his idea to erect a skyscraper, the tallest building in Boston, and with an observation desk on Clarendon Street.

John shook his head. "You sure did yourself no favors with the Douglas case. Ain't saying I don't appreciate what you did for my folks. An entire police department is aching for an excuse to shoot you on sight. Helluva accomplishment for a white boy. Doesn't add up? With two stiffs in the morgue, you're adding up to become number three."

I shot John another look. Tired, I focused back on the road. "We're almost there."

It was winter. I had amped up the heat, and John was perspiring. Passive-aggressive of me. I smiled when I looked into the mirror and saw his long fingers wipe away a bead of sweat that rolled out of his sideburn. "Hope this Bill is as good a friend as you say he is."

"He is. And don't forget I said he's different."

"If he's white, then he ain't no different to me. No offense intended."

"None taken."

I came to a complete stop and showed him.

John didn't mind the idea of walking into a gay bar. What he objected to was the name of the establishment. "Man, you've got to be kidding me." I ducked my head down to read the marquee through the windshield.

John was apoplectic. "The Ramrod? The joint is called The Ramrod!"

The bar had a Victorian vibe to it for an exterior, as in this side of Jekyll and Hyde and Jack the Ripper. By day, it was a bland set of doors, which, like any other thruway in Boston, is where people stepped inside to light a match, swap drugs for cash, or, for the more intrepid, quick sex against a wall. Come nighttime, the place got garish.

Before Bill frequented here, the club had a dress code of dungarees with tee shirt and boots, or naked once inside. Sex was as rampant as ants at a picnic.

Upstairs. Downstairs. In the bathrooms, in the hallways.

One guy, Bill explained, owned a pair of what Bill called 'Mine Shaft dungarees.' The knees on them were black from crawling around on the floor. No matter how much he washed them, the stains wouldn't come out. I told John I needed to find parking and also said, "One more thing."

"What?"

"Don't let someone pick you up."

The look I received from John required no subtitle or translation. I put up with the slow creep-around of other cars in search of a parking spot, drivers behind the wheel and glass cursing me, while John got out of the car.

I found a spot, cut the wheel several times to parallel-park John's gold Cutlass. I climbed out, keys in hand to admire my work. The car's paintjob, advertised as Saturn Gold, reminded me of bowling balls at Sacco's in Somerville.

Before John left, I'd given him the particulars on how to ID Bill in the crowd. Five minutes in, I found them both. Bill was dressed like a strumpet with a heart of brass in tight leather pants, airy pirate shirt, and gold loop in his right ear. The short leather jacket with ratty fur collar completed the ensemble. John sat on Bill's right. I sat opposite them.

"We need answers, Bill," I said.

"We?" he said, giving John the once-over. "I can't say we've been properly introduced." Bill extended his hand, and John looked at it as if it were a dirty dishcloth, but shook it anyway, and introduced himself.

A leather-boy approached our table. I took in the sight. About five-eight, in black leather pants, no shirt, a vest and a hat with a chinstrap below a thick, black moustache. He was not what the Pagan's Motorcycle Club would've recruited during their membership drive.

"Coke, smoke, or dope?" he asked.

"No thanks," I said.

His eyes took an active interest in John, sweeping those searchlights over his torso. "Poppers, perhaps?"

"Man said no," John said in a baritone voice à la Barry White.

"Wait," I said, noticing an inebriated man at pinball machine across the room. He seemed familiar to me. Frustrated, he lifted the machine off its legs to work the pinball. "Who is he?" Our hospitality boy sighed. "Bruins player. A teddy bear and a gentleman, but a real sad sack once he passes his limit."

"I don't see any drinks on the machine."

"The bar cut him off an hour ago. All part of the agreement."

"Agreement between him and the bar?" I asked.

"I shouldn't talk, but there's an understanding between his manager and the owner. Our pinball wizard gets a set number of drinks, the use of the back rooms, and then a limo takes him home. Nice arrangement, if you ask me."

"Who's his manager?" I tried to find a bill to tip him in the darkness, but he stopped me. "Honey, I can't take your money for something I don't know. You want to know? Ask him."

He walked away to hawk his wares.

"Hear that music?" Bill said. "A customer brought this back from Munich, a bootleg LP. Donna Summer. She's a South End girl, or was before she moved to Europe."

"Love to Love You Baby" bled through the sound system. Bill had his facts half-right. Donna Summer had been born in Boston, raised in Mission Hill, and sang in a church in the South End. A story circulated she fled to Europe after she'd witnessed a murder, and feared for her life. No idea if the rumor was true.

"Love this," Bill said, shoulders shimming to the singer's moans.

"Bill?" I reached over the table and stopped the shoulders with firm hands.

"What's the news around the house?"

"I don't know it word for word, but someone at the station said you visited Savitz at his office, asking all kinds of questions about Roger Sherman. You threatened him."

"I threatened him? What did his secretary say?"

"What secretary?" Bill resumed his movement to the music. I saw John's impatient eyes. I lit into Bill again.

"Did Savitz say anything about Roger or Bay Village?"

"No."

I raked old ground. "What about your partner?"

"Who?" Bill cupped his ear. "I can't hear you."

I grabbed hold of some pirate shirt and pulled Bill closer. "Listen to me. I talked to Jimmy, like you asked. I went to Bay Village, like you asked. Favor for a friend, like you asked. I meet a cop and I had a welcome party. What about your partner?"

"We talked about him," Bill answered, disgusted. His mouth twisted into a sneer. John placed his hand on Bill's shoulder and pulled him close so he could talk to Bill.

"Your friend here told me he took the case in front of your partner, a cop. Shane checked Roger's place. Cop showed up. He researches a lead on Savitz from Jimmy, and lo and behold, cops were on him again, but for murder this time."

Bill tried to pry John's hand off his shoulder. "Then talk to Jimmy."

Bill squeezed harder. "You gave Jimmy to Mr. Cleary. Remember? Your friend was working a paying case before he did you a favor and, in working on the case that pays, cops appear on Beacon Hill and later, outside the Little Building. Coincidences? I think not."

"Now you think I had something to do with it?"

"How did the cops know to show up at Dunbar's?" I asked.

"The accountant?" Bill seemed flummoxed. "Somebody could've heard the shot."

"I was out cold, Bill."

Bill looked stunned, as if a mule had kicked him. "You think I set you up?"

The singer's cooing grated on my nerves. I wanted the girl to make it over the edge, and have her orgasm. I wanted answers from Bill.

"I trusted you, Bill, but look at things from where I'm sitting. I put away a crooked cop, and the constituency wants me dead. I own that, but this other stuff with Sherman and Savitz? I need to know what you know because you're on the inside, and the Barbarian is involved somehow."

"I don't know anything, I swear."

Donna Summer whimpered while Bill huffed frustration. Bill lost interest in his latest acoustic joy. John stared into the dark room.

"I've got to get a leash on the Barbarian," I said.

"What do you suggest?" Bill asked.

"Talk to the Italians."

"Are you nuts, man?" John's head turned so fast, bones should've cracked.

"Why not?" I said. "The way I see it, the mob has their rules, and I've got to believe they're not happy when one of their own goes off the reservation. We should see if they do take care of their own. I've got an idea, but we can discuss it tomorrow. I've got to do something first."

The dance floor crowd jostled me around. John and Bill followed, not clear on the mission. I brushed past one guy who wanted a kiss. Colored lights pulsated everywhere. Specks of white from a mirrored ball strafed the floor and the walls.

I approached the jingle of the pinball hitting bells, the clatter of points ratcheting up the score. Flippers clicked, the man grunted feral sounds as he humped the machine like a lover. The ball arced off a ramp with too much speed and shot wide as a gutter ball. Game over.

"Impressive score," I said. The man wasn't tall, but he wasn't short either. Built like a badger, he had rosacea on his cheeks, which he covered with a touch of foundation. His eyes were glassy.

"I don't mean to intrude, but a friend of mine would love to have you drop in for an appearance for the kids. Charity. I heard you like helping out kids."

"Every chance I get," he said. "I've been a part of a hockey camp for the little ones for years. I tried to start one for young girls. Equality, you know, but my agent nixed the idea, said the association with women's lib wasn't the right kind of publicity."

"Guy sounds like Archie Bunker," I said.

"Ain't that the half of it?" His hand dug deep into jeans tight enough I could count the change in his pockets. "Saying no to the man is like saying no to the devil." He sorted through change he salvaged from his right pocket. He must've felt the need for casual patter because he made small talk. "Did you know pinball is illegal in New York? A form of gambling, they claim."

He put his change on the counter, reached behind for his wallet. "Ask your friend, the one with the charity, to contact my agent." He handed me the business card. "Call that number and talk to his secretary. She'll call you back if he approves."

"That controlling?"

"He counts the breaths I take. Guy even has the bartender here on his payroll."

"Thanks for the card," I said and put change from my pocket on the glass surface.

***

We found the door and said bye to the place as Gloria Gaynor started in on last year's "Never Can Say Goodbye." John said not one word while we walked to the car. About two steps away from his golden chariot, he and Bill both stopped. "What's the plan?" John asked.

"Why, are you in?" I asked.

"I'm in," John answered and turned to Bill. Bill nodded. "I'm in."

I held up the business card so the two of them could see it. Bill squinted and read the name and occupation. "Marty Savitz, Agent."

"Son of a bitch." John's breath ghosted in the cold winter air.

I unlocked the doors, forgetting to ask Bill about his unofficial homicide case.

Chapter 17: Angles

I visited Bill the next morning alone. I went to make amends. He had the day off, and I showed up just as Mr. Coffee dropped his last drop into the pot. "Morning," I said.

"Black, right?"

I said yes as I peeled off my jacket. I saw a lump of clay on the counter. Bill had jumped onto the hand-strengthening craze after seeing the movie *The Mechanic*. Charles Bronson worked a handful of clay throughout the film. The actor, whom I remembered mostly from westerns, played a hit man mentoring the fair-haired Jan-Michael Vincent, an actor who made women and some men swoon.

"Play-Doh," I said and picked up the ball of clay. "I remembered this stuff from when I was little." I put it to my nose. The odor was distinctive and far safer than sniffing glue. I had friends from my days in foster care who'd become huffers. It'd started innocently enough, with putting together model airplanes and cars.

Bill handed me a mug. I put the ball down on the counter and said, "Loved the smell of this stuff. About last night, I meant for us talk about your homicide case."

"After what you said, save it."

"Don't be like that, Bill."

I stood and Bill sat on a stool. The idea of a kitchen nook was alien to me. A table belonged either in a kitchen or a dining room. A nook reminded me of the saloon bar, a deli counter, or something we stole from Eskimos.

"Look, before we talk," Bill said, "I need you to be straight with me."

"No problem."

I had an idea where this was headed, but right now I wasn't sure of anything. Dunbar was dead. The Barbarian had almost killed me and I hadn't a clue whether he, or any of the pieces of this mess, was connected to Bray.

"When you called me for a sheet on Dunbar, you said it was for a case. You said you were working the angles. Remember?"

I'd let him practice. Bill was using the Socratic method to work me into a mousetrap.

"I recall the conversation," I said. "I said 'angles', or words to that effect."

"Last night your friend John mentioned cops at Dunbar's, and cops outside the Little Building."

"Which you said you knew nothing about. Cut to the chase, Bill, and ask your question."

I had to admit it: Bill impressed me. He had excellent recall, and concentration. He was off-hours now, his day off and a time when he should've been kicking back and relaxing. Most cops needed down-time, but a detective was always on the clock, always alert and observant. The habit, the vigilance, worked itself into a groove in everything you did, and how you viewed the world and people around you. Family. Friends. Perps.

Bill didn't distract easily. Donna Summer may have been crooning last night, but Bill was a red-blooded American male, even if he played for the other team. Last night, he'd been surrounded by his element. He should've been distracted, but wasn't.

"John said 'paying one' as in 'original gig,' by which he meant Dunbar, right?"

"Correct," I said, though technically, the money came from Bray, and Dunbar had been the initial lead from the client. The real clue for me was the Xerox on the third floor, and there was no connection between Dunbar and that machine. Whatever evidence Dunbar had disappeared with his killer and what I had for ledgers after the encounter with the Barbarian was luck and more of the same evidence.

I hadn't touched my coffee. Bill asked if it was okay, though not because he was worried about its quality. He used the question to distract me, to lull me into false comfort before he asked his real question. His hand worked the lump of Play-Doh.

"Who is the client that required a background on Dunbar?"

There it was. Out in the morning sunshine with two fresh mugs of coffee.

"Brayton and Cat Braddock. I'm working a case for Brayton."

The sentence hung in the air. I watched Bill. He shook his head. His hand throttled the clay. I knew I deserved whatever was coming next. Bill knew of Cat and our history together.

"Jesus, Shane. You can't stay away from her, can you?"

"I said the job was for her husband."

Bill relaxed his hand, the lump of clay still in his palm. I was surprised he hadn't thrown it at me.

"Mark my words, Shane Cleary. She has something to do with your case and Dunbar. I don't know how, but that woman is a biblical plague for you. Locusts here, frogs there, and one day, the Angel of Death."

"Done with the religious imagery and melodrama? If you are, then let's talk about your case with the douche husband."

We reviewed basics first. She, the deceased, had filed the papers for divorce. He'd moved out of their apartment. Bill said phone records indicate the couple kept in touch. Nobody, however, could say whether their exchanges over the phone had been acrimonious. Friends and family made statements that the couple had a contentious marriage. He was Stanley Kowalski to her Stella.

There was no Blanche in the picture that the Homicide detectives could find, nor any new beau in the dead wife's life either. Bill and I went over the DDs, the incidents of domestic disputes. Our Stanley had a few restraining orders against him. None violated.

He stopped and smiled. Bill had something on the husband and seemed eager to walk up to the front of the class and read his report.

"You told me to establish a timeline on this guy," Bill said. "I talked to neighbors and they did see the jerk on occasion, but no arguments. You mentioned SOS to me. We talked about distress signals, and then I started thinking sex."

"Were there any signs of sex?"

"Neighbors said he'd stayed overnight on occasion, but none of the neighborhood snoops could place him in or near the apartment at the time of the murder. The ME's Report, which finally came in, did say the body showed SOS but nothing violent."

Bill and I stopped for sips of coffee.

"Consensual then," I said. "A defense attorney for this mope will argue a lack of motive, even claims an attempt at reconciliation, especially if the ME matches semen to the night she died. An alibi?"

Bill's face crinkled. "He said he was playing poker with friends."

"There's something else bothering you. What? I can tell from the look on your face."

"He used a rubber, but the husband doesn't deny sexual relations."

"Simple," I said. "Ask him when was the last time he slept with her."

"His statement to the detectives says he was with her a day or two before her death." I shook my head. His turn to ask, "What?"

"Prick knows sperm survives one to two days after its launched. Lawyer will argue reasonable doubt, unless you break his timeline. Did you check for insurance?"

"The Great Pyramid was built faster, although her sister said she had a life insurance policy, but didn't know details. Anecdotal, I say, and policies are cancelled and amended all the time."

I listened to the rest of Bill's report. The Medical Examiner had established a time of death. The husband said he was playing poker, his usual night and time. Homicide verified the game, talked to the players, and even had notes on the play-by-play that led to the winning hand and taking the pot. Nothing broke the bastard's timeline.

I swallowed hard when Bill's grin widened. "What? You've got something?"

"It's not solid, but hear me out. Remember I said her hair was wet?"

"Yeah, but how does that break hubby's alibi?"

"I worked angles of my own on this case. I went to the scene after I reviewed all the photographs. Husband's fingerprints were all over the place, which means nothing since we've established they'd been intimate."

"Okay," I said. "Walk me through motive and means from the top."

"Let's assume there was an insurance policy. Motive. Let's also assume his poker buddies are loyal to a fault, or that he'd promised them a cut of the insurance money. That makes them accomplices."

"Or suspects to lean on to break husband's alibi," I said.

"Even better," Bill said. "It's a stretch but these guys all share two things in common: bitter divorces and substantial alimony payments. A stretch, yes, which takes me back to her shower before she died."

Bill savored his next sip of coffee. I sensed not a shoe, but a piano whistling through the air for Wiley E. Coyote on the sidewalk.

"I'm listening."

"Photographs from the crime scene show the door to the bathroom was open. Nothing extraordinary about that, right? You said to me once that detectives recreate the crime scene in their heads; they walk themselves through the scene, thinking as either victim or criminal."

"I did, and what do you see, Bill."

"Here's how I think it played out: she expected hubby to come over for a roll in the hay. Evidence supports that assumption. She was found not wearing a lot of clothes. They had sex, but here is where the evidence doesn't add up for me. Women put on makeup, a touch of lipstick; they pretty themselves up, put on lingerie, but she takes a shower?"

"He's seen her a million times without makeup, and some people shower before sex."

"But let's assume she suspected that he was going to kill her. She takes a long, hot shower, closes the door even, but then leaves it open when she's done."

I had the coffee mug halfway to my mouth when Bill stopped talking. He stared at me, placid and patient.

"You're killing me here, Bill. Say it."

"What happens when you take a prolonged shower?"

"I don't know. You get wet. There's steam."

"That's right, there's steam," Bill said. "Steam that fades away, when you leave the door open. What doesn't go away is if you wrote something on the mirror and don't wipe it down."

I smiled. "You didn't."

"I did. I cranked the shower until I had myself a sauna and then I waited and watched that mirror as the bathroom aired out. She'd written on the mirror. She named him and it gets better."

I waited.

"She dated and timed her message. I repeated my little experiment for Homicide. They're going to pick him up and see what they get out of him."

I raised my mug for a toast. "You'll make a fine detective, Bill."

Chapter 18: Wonderland

"I never understood the appeal of this place," Bill said from the back seat of John's car.

I had sliced the Cutlass over two white lines and sailed into the lot, where gravel and grit tickled the underside of the car. I killed the radio and engine. I might've mumbled something, like "take me out to the ball game," but this was not that kind of park. Bill had made that much clear.

The place was a dog track, Wonderland in Revere. Some gangsters are inveterate gamblers. They took chances with their lives, with the lives of those around them, and they'd bet outrageous sums on the stupidest shit. I've seen hoods in the back of a restaurant, after they'd collected extortion money, race lobsters on the floor. The winning crustacean received a temporary reprieve from the boiling pot. I never understood gambling, no more than I understood why anyone would put a jacket on a greyhound and bet hard-earned cash to watch the poor animal chase a mechanical rabbit around a track. The Chinese had their mahjong. Blacks had the Numbers. The Irish and Italian threw dice, sharped cards, or bet on dogs and ponies.

We stayed close, once out of John's car. The Barbarian was sure to be around, but I wasn't there for him. I was in the court of Mr. B, the reigning don of Boston's North End. It didn't take me long to spot him in the stands. The aquiline nose and the balding head gave him away. The two gorilla bodyguards didn't help.

Mr. B's nickname was Pinky, but nobody dared call him that to his face. He traced his pedigree to Prohibition. As a kid, he ran gin and then managed the largest juniper operation in the country. Mr. B was the last of the Italian bosses left standing after the wars with the Irish. Since Mr. B was a hundred-percent Italian, he was eligible for membership to the real club. Their Sicilian thing, Cosa Nostra, had conceded Boston to the Irish on the sole condition they share business with Mr. B. He was the plum Italian tomato staked in the garden. The other Italian mobsters had relocated to Rhode Island.

I approached and one of his henchmen stood up. I showed my hands. I sat down next to Mr. B., and John took the bench in front of him. Another goon sat behind me. Bill took the seat next to him.

"Afternoon, Mr. B. Do you know who I am?"

"Yeah, I know who you are. A mick friend of mine told me about you. What do you want, Mr. Cleary?"

"I have a problem."

"Take a number and get in line."

The announcer garbled something over the PA. The masses moved inside to the windows to place their bets at the cages. Mr. B's entourage didn't move. They itched to bet but they stayed put, next to their boss.

"My problem goes to the front of the line," I said.

"Says who?"

"Hear me out first and I think you'll agree with me when I'm done. My problem is the Barbarian. Now, the look on your face says you don't care, but you should, and I'll get to why in a minute. Last I heard through the grapevine, he had been packed off to San Francisco, but since he's back in town that must mean one of two things. A, he's here to do a job that either nobody wants or that only he can pull off, or B, his personality so charmed your colleagues on the left coast that they expressed-mailed him back, free of charge. Is it A or B?"

"B."

Bettors hugged the fence, betting slips in hand. In the distance I saw the canine thoroughbreds seed the stalls. Greyhounds are nice dogs, majestic, quite the loungers and patient, too. We betray their gentle disposition with this atrocious sport.

Mr. B asked, "Who's the eggplant?"

John turned his head, rage in his eyes. He sat there and took it, though. Mr.

B was standard five-seven or five-eight. He dressed with a little flair, but not too much. He chose good material for his winter coat and his scarf was something a commoner would wear on a cold day. Money didn't go to his head or soften his waist. He didn't stop with John.

"And what's with Tinker Bell with the earring behind us?" he asked.

"I'm glad you're interested in my friends, Pinky." That got me a sideways glare, but he knew I had to defend them somehow. He gave me the tight smile. We understood each other.

"Mr. Black in front of you is the proprietor of a pool hall. Central Square. The gentleman behind you is one of Boston's finest." Mr. B flinched a tight acknowledgment to John and Bill.

"You know," he said to me, "I wonder how you sit down with those big balls you've got. Why should I give a damn about you and your pals here?"

"You should care because the Barbarian is freelancing. He shook down Mr. Black here for a pretty penny, and it isn't even his territory, and I'll bet that you didn't get one dime of tribute." I turned my attention to John and asked him. "How much did he take you for, Mr. Black?"

"Two grand, and next month it's twenty-one hundred. There isn't even any protection to go with it from that mother—excuse me, your business associate."

"See that, Mr. B?" I said. "My friend here understands there's a cost to doing business, but it usually involves some kind of exchange. Your colleague is running his own shop, by his own rules, which tells me there's a lack of respect, a lack of structure in your organization, and zero loyalty to you. Mr. Black's situation isn't the only independent venture your boy is running these days."

"He's not my boy," Mr. B said.

"Oh, I was mistaken then. I was under the impression your people had guidelines, and that was what separated you from other businessmen. Mr. Black is plantation Negro. Me? I'm cut-glass Irish. My pal behind us is excommunicated and damned to hell, for reasons we don't have to spell out. But you, Mr. B, you're descended from the ancient Romans."

The starter pistol cracked the air, the rabbit released. The dogs galloped through the downs in pursuit, throwing up cakes of mud behind them.

Mr. B asked in a low voice. "He's running another show?"

"Real estate," I said.

"I don't believe it. He's all muscle and no brains. The man is an illiterate."

"Could be, but he was smart enough to siphon money without your knowing it. Who knows how much he is milking from the bars and strip clubs in the Zone. We both know they pay protection money."

We looked at each other. He didn't like the idea of someone licking his piece of candy first. "Do you have any proof he's into real estate?"

"I do. I have ledgers, and there's more. I know he's involved because he was interested enough to make an appearance at the O.K. Corral." Mr. B gave me an odd look, so I elaborated. "The Barbarian, the incident at the Little Building. I'm sure you heard about it. He was there and so were cops, who gave him permission. I know how you and your friends like free publicity."

Mr. B's jaw tensed before he said, "Stupid son of a bitch always did draw attention to himself. These ledgers you mentioned, what's special about them?"

"You know anything about a major real estate deal in town?" I asked.

"I might. I can't stop it, you know. Damn thing is huge."

"I appreciate your candor. No, you can't stop it, but I bet you have some say about who gets what among your countrymen in the construction business. The Barbarian isn't management material, but there's no reason not to think he won't dip his paw into the till and take a percentage. He's a grunt and nothing more, you said so yourself, in so many words. You don't like it when people think above their pay-grade. Am I right?"

"Keep talking," he said.

"Well, the ledgers are part of a series, sets of books, as in master and dummy. Familiar with the concept?" Mr. B said nothing. I continued. "Nothing illegal about, but I'll wager money the masters tell the true story of all the parties involved, and the dummy set was written for dummies. One has to wonder what would happen if both sets of ledgers found their way into the hands of federal and state auditors."

"What parties are we talking about here?" he asked.

"WASPS, the people with buckles on their hats. The next wave of politicos are in league with them, which is bad for you, because they write the laws. The nice thing about your colleague, the one with no brains, is he probably made himself their muscle for cash on the barrel, and for a slice of territory he could call his own. I'd leave it you to guess the zip code and what that means for you, if they protect him."

Mr. B didn't like what he was hearing. His pale blue eyes seemed to turn to a merciless shade of gray. His exhalation in the cold air came out in one long plume. The winning dog was announced, but Mr. B wasn't interested.

"How do I know you're not making this all up? You've got nothing to lose from where I'm sitting. The police are after you for at least two murders."

"You're absolutely right, so take your chances then."

I made to get up, but his hand seized my elbow.

"Sit down. What is it that you want and what are you offering?"

"I'll give you the ledgers in good faith. I have them in my friend's car. There are others, but I can't get to them. I have no doubt you can find the rest of them, though. What you do with them is your business, but my friends here have been loyal, and I wouldn't be any kind of leader if I didn't advocate on their behalf before I said what I wanted in exchange. Are you open to what I have to say?"

"I'm listening," he said.

"Mr. Black deserves reparations, but he'll be happy to hear an assurance from you that he won't receive any more visits from the Barbarian. He's paying two pipers, so I ask you that it either be you or the Winter Hill gang, but not both. I believe Mr. Black would prefer doing business with you, but it's your decision since you have to pull the Barbarian off Mr. Black. My friend behind you works the dog shift. It'd like to see him get a slot to take the detective's exam."

"And you? What do you want?"

"An uninterrupted moment with the Barbarian."

"Listen, my Irish friend, do you really think it would be wise to be alone with him? He'll maim you first and then eat your liver before he kills you."

"I'll take my chances."

Mr. B eyes stared into the distance for a moment. "You're offering a lot to get close to the Barbarian. I don't get it. What's your cut in all of this?"

"A Q and A with the Barbarian, and I'd like to consider the ledgers as an insurance policy."

The worry lines in Mr. B's forehead lifted. "Insurance?"

"In case something happens to me." I shifted my rear on the bench to square myself with the man. "Reach into my jacket," I said. "My wallet is on your right."

His eyes squinted in suspicion. I encouraged him again. He bypassed the holster. His left hand found the pocket and pulled out my wallet and opened it. He saw the PI license.

"Take the first business card," I said. "I wrote down an address where I think you'll find the rest of those ledgers. Keep the card. Feel I've been dishonest, you know where to find me. After I talk with your colleague, send him back to San Francisco, take care of him your way. I don't care."

"You don't want the satisfaction?"

"All I want is a moment with him before he swims out west."

Mr. B asked one of his cronies for a pen. He had taken two more business cards from my billfold. He wrote on the back of the first card. "Come back here tomorrow at this time."

He wrote something on the back of the second card. He handed that card to John. "It's something for your troubles, Mr. Black. My monthly rate is far less than what you're paying, and you'll get something for your money. Do business with me, and you have my word nobody in Southie or from Somerville will bother you. Ever."

The two men shook hands.

Mr. B looked over his shoulder and asked for Bill's badge number. Bill said it. Mr. B didn't write that down, but he did tell Bill. "I'll take care of it."

"Now, about those ledgers?" he asked me.

Bill volunteered and I gave him the keys. We watched Bill scamper off to the parking lot. Mr. B said, "Tomorrow, one of my men will take you inside the clubhouse. You'll find the Barbarian there. Wait until he goes to the lavatory. Private and less of a scene. You have your moment with him there, and you'll owe me one for getting Tinker Bell a chair for the detective's exam."

"Understood," I said, and I had to ask because it bothered me. "What's the appeal in dog racing?"

Mr. B shrugged. "Tradition. I've been coming to Wonderland since I was a kid. I don't even like dogs. I don't hate them, but they're a lot of work, like kids. I much prefer cats."

"Me too."

Bill returned with the ledgers. He had push behind him to take the detective's exam now. John had money in his pocket and a different community liaison. I had a conversation booked for tomorrow. I had one last question for my benefactor.

"What would you do if someone were blackmailing a sports figure that made you money?"

"What do you think?"

"Even if said athlete were homosexual?"

"I'm a liberal man, Mr. Cleary. I don't care where and with whom my money sleeps so long as my interest is warm, protected, and keeps making me more money." Mr. B rose and secured a stray button.

"Too bad the guy they found in the Fens didn't share your views," I said.

"Terrible thing what happened to him." The old don shook his head. "Terrible thing."

Chapter 19: The Animal

John packed the cash from the cage window, thanks to Mr. B, inside the glove compartment. I suggested he wait for me in the car.

"Am I your chauffeur now?" he asked.

"It's a mobbed-up clubhouse, John. Stay in the car, please."

"I see, buses and school districts aren't the only things segregated in this town."

It was a new trio at Wonderland the next day: me and Bill, and one of Mr. B's handymen, a no-neck with jowls and hooded eyes who yodeled his Boston accent between wheezes. He didn't cotton to winter well. His name was Tony Two-Times for the habit of clicking his lighter twice when he lit up a cigarette.

"I gotta hand it to you, Cleary, you've got stones," he said, halfway through the crunch of hard mud and the confetti of torn tickets. The man wore a coat of sweat on his forehead. "The Barbarian is an animal." He stopped me with his pudgy, ungloved hand. I looked down at it. "I mean it. The guy is a real animal. He bites."

Bill overhead. "Are you serious?"

"Dead serious." The fat man narrowed his eyes and put his face close to mine. His breath smelled of nail polish. "Ever see his teeth? That son of a bitch didn't even smile at his mother the day he was born. Only time that dreg breaks a grin is when he's putting a bullet into someone's hat. Dog teeth is what you'll find." He flexed his lips into a sneer for me. "His canines are pointy like a vampire's."

He jabbed his finger into my shoulder to emphasize his next point. "Don't let the bastard get close to you because he'll take whatever he can get. I saw him bite a man's nose off once."

We resumed our constitutional. Tony Two-Times continued the Marlin Perkins from *Wild Kingdom* narrative. "Most people don't know it, but if you chomp a man's nose off, he'll bleed to death, or choke to death on his own blood. Not much you can do about it unless you catheterize the beak in time."

"Don't you mean cauterize?" I said.

"That's what I said."

"Charming," Bill said, behind me.

"Yeah, charming is right," Tony said. "That's the Barbarian for you."

Our bonhomie ended at the foot of the stairs up to the clubhouse. The steps were iced and the wooden railing about as treacherous. Tony explained the layout and set expectations as we climbed the staircase. The front of the clubhouse was for those in search of suds, dogs on a bun slathered with some kind of goodness, and salted pretzels warm enough to pull apart like taffy.

Inside the clubhouse, the clientele were high rollers, people who wanted and paid a subscription for privacy. I thought of Roger and the house in Bay Village. This clubhouse had a back room, the size of a ballroom. I've always been suspicious of back rooms. Sure, big money schemes were planned and hatched there, but most back rooms were the last four walls a guy saw. He'd enjoy his last meal there before the gun behind his ear. Abandoned car lots throughout Revere, in and around Logan Airport, told the same story.

Smallish television sets broadcasted OTB from Manhattan, and one set played the local news station. Tables filled the room, silverware shone, including princess forks for shrimp arranged around the rims of cocktail glasses.

Tony and I separated. He said that he'd act casual, make the rounds, and then make himself invisible. Bill and I stayed in a darkened corner behind the water boys. Tony Two-Times had an unexpected grace about him. I saw him turn sideways this way to make way for couples and that way for waiters and food trays. He squeezed himself between chairs without so much as disrupting the safe passage of fork to mouth for diners.

I watched the meet and greet.

The Barbarian rose, shook hands, and introduced his guest, an airline stewardess still in uniform. Blonde, tall, the colors of her outfit said she was a Pan Am girl. She was on an obvious layover and she and the Barbarian seemed to enjoy more than table trays in the upright position. Tony patted the Barbarian on the shoulder when he made his goodbye. Tony's eyes met mine. It was now the Army's hurry-up and wait for a man's bladder.

The Barbarian didn't drink. He confined his choice of libations to water. Smart. His girlfriend du jour soaked up martinis. The water brigade converged on his emptied glass with their pitchers. The Barbarian rose, excused himself for the head. He walked there with a limp.

The way his arms moved, the Barbarian had unbuttoned his blazer. It could mean he readied his fly, or access to his weapon. I tailed him with Bill in tow. The one palpable worry I had was that someone would stop the man. Any bottleneck here, any chance that the man might turn around, meant death. I might've chipped his shin the last time we met, but he'd tap my heart and head with whatever he carried inside his two-button wool sport coat. I drifted leftward of the hallway when he took the narrow passage in case he looked over his shoulder for a shadow. Bill followed my lead and hid.

I counted one Mississippi, two Mississippi until I reached five and went in. I found him at the urinal. Bill pasted his back to the door. The Barbarian laughed to himself and glanced down while he sprayed the mothballs.

"Are you two nimrods planning to Dutch Schultz me? Huh? Are you gonna shoot me, like they shot him while he was taking a leak in Newark? Some fucking nerve, you two."

I placed myself near the stalls. He had his hands south of the equator still and all I cared about was whether they went north of the belt. He shook himself, twitched a leg and zipped up, doing an up-and-down jingle. I would've laughed if it had been anyone else, but not this lunatic. I leaned against an opened stall door on my left.

He indicated the sink. "May I?"

I said nothing. He limped his way to the sink. He jammed the palm of his right hand twice under the pink soap globe. His left hand turned on the water. He kept his eyes on me through my reflection in the mirror above the sink. The sound of a flush surprised us both. I didn't turn my head, though. We heard a latch pull and a stall door open. The Barbarian looked up in the mirror and spoke to the reflection. "So Tony Two-Times is in on this party with these two mooks?"

"I'm not with them. I'm here at Mr. B's request. I'm just an observer."

"Yeah, and you're a U.N. delegate."

Tony chose a washbasin three down from the Barbarian. He did his wash-up.

"So Tony...since when does Mr. B listen to a washed-up mick and a faggot?"

Both men had turned off their water and flicked their hands of excess moisture. Paper towels were piled on a ledge above the sinks. The Barbarian took a handful. Tony took a handful. The near-synchronicity, while not water ballet, impressed me.

Tony Two-Times crumpled paper towels and tossed them into the trash. He chose a wall and crossed his arms. The Barbarian dried his hands, too. He then crumpled the paper in them. The wad of paper landed at my feet.

"Talk to him, Joe." Tony indicated me. The Barbarian had a first name.

"Screw him, Tony. I want to hear it from you."

"Not my place, Joe. I'm here as a third-party, at Mr. B's request, like I said. You have anything to say, direct it at Mr. Cleary here."

"Mr. Cleary, is it? I remember you. Little Building."

The Barbarian parted his blazer. Double-holster on one side. He wore a Browning auto under his left armpit and under that a smaller gun, a .22 for the finishing touch. He took another step, to test boundaries while my hand rested on the top edge of a stall door.

"What have you got to say to me, Mr. Cleary?"

"Simple question. Who do you work for?"

He cracked his knuckles, one by one, while he talked. "Just like that, you think I'm gonna tell you my business. You want to know what my answer is to that? Two words. Guess what they are."

"Have it your way," I told him. "Here's a newsflash for you, Joe. You're going back to San Francisco. You have friends there from what I've been told.

You can sit with your girlfriend, the stewardess, or you can take your seat in cargo. I'm certain they can fit you into a nice suitcase or two, or three."

"You're dreaming, my stupid mick friend."

I didn't turn to see Tony's reaction. The Barbarian and I were now eye to eye. I didn't move my head and give him an ear. I stared back at him. His eyes darted to Tony Two-Times. "San Francisco? Is he snowing me?"

"I'm afraid not."

The Barbarian made his move. I swung the stall door to meet his fist. I heard a loud crack. He held his right hand and howled in pain. He tried to punch me again, but I had dodged the blow. Rookie move on his part to expose his flank. I peppered his ribs on one side, slammed him against the stall. A girl's move, but I kicked his bad shin. He reached for a handful of hair with his left hand. I saw the mouth yawn open.

Tony Two-Times was right. The Barbarian had pointy canines. I hammered his midsection. His right hand reached. I grabbed the wrist. There's no way I would let his hand approach either gun. My knee upward placed his jewels higher up the family tree and, when he lurched forward in agony, I brought my elbow down hard on a shoulder blade first and then the back of his head.

He surged backwards. I lost the wrist, but got his head inside the V of my left arm. I winched my wrist hard. He gasped for air and stomped his foot around for the instep of my foot. He did what he could with his elbows. We pin-wheeled into a stall where his blue face read the graffiti.

"Tell me who you work for?" I asked him.

He didn't answer me, so I slammed his face into the wall. I asked again. Nothing. I rammed his head into the metal divider again. The wall buckled. The crazy bastard started laughing through blood and snot. I decided that it was time to clean him up. I drove his head down into the toilet bowl.

"Who do you work for? Is it Braddock?" I had his face an inch above the drink. No answer. He went down for a rinse. I yanked him up and asked him again.

"I don't know anybody named Braddock," he said between coughs and sputters.

"Wrong answer," I said and jammed his head into the baptismal water. I didn't count any Mississippis. I yanked his head up. An arc of water came up with him and splashed me. I yelled into his ear, "When did Braddock hire you out?"

"I told you I don't know no Braddock. You deaf or something?"

I sank him again, headfirst. I held him down until his legs squirmed. I hit the lever for a flush and reeled him up after the bowl cleared.

The Barbarian spat out water. "Son of a bitch."

"Who booked you for this gig?"

He twisted his head enough to give me a sneer. "You really want to know?"

I readied him for another rinse and repeat when he said, "Okay, okay,"

"Who?"

"There was no guy, I swear."

"Who then?"

"A woman. A broad hired me."

I almost sagged when I heard that. "To do what?"

"Find books. Accounting stuff. She paid me fifty K."

I banged his head against the stall. "You're lying."

"Swear on my mother."

"When did she hire you?"

"I don't know. Do I look like I carry a day planner to you?"

"Wiseass." I grabbed him by the throat, waited until his eyes bulged before I loosened my grip. "When?" I asked.

"Relax, will yeah? Two weeks ago. She hired me two weeks ago."

I grabbed him by his wet lapels. "How did all this go down?"

"She called me, said to meet her at the Copley Square Hotel. She sent over her driver to take me there. Man, she was some dish."

I didn't want to hear the rest, but the Barbarian wouldn't spare me.

"She pulled out all the stops. I never knew a woman could smell so nice. She gave it up in the penthouse suite. I never had it so—"

I punched him. Hard. He doubled over. "Skip that part. Tell me about the job."

"She hired me to find ledgers. I did and I made copies of them for her, like she asked. I offered to steal them for her, but she said that would arouse

136

suspicion."

"You found the books. You made copies. Then what?" I said.

"I called her. Her driver swung by my place and picked me up. I met with her, handed her the goods right there in the car, and that's when I told her there was a consultant named Dunbar looking into her husband's books."

Stunned. "You had her number?"

He nodded, rose and rested against the stall. "Private line. Wrote her digits on the back of some card myself, but I lost it."

While he ran his tongue against his teeth, to see if they were all there, I reached into my pocket and produced the business card. I turned it over, phone number facing him. "Is this the card?"

"Yeah, and that's my writing. Satisfied now?"

"No," I said. "Last question. Why did you show up at the Little Building? Guns blazing."

"That was fun, wasn't it?"

"Hilarious." I cocked my fist and he flinched. "Answer the question."

"After Dunbar was killed, she called me and told me to get whatever books I could find, and that's what I tried to do but I ran into you and Einstein."

Floored, I said, "So you didn't kill Dunbar?"

"I might be crazy, but I'm not nuts. She's got brains, that one. No photocopies this time," he said, and I must've look as if it didn't register. He enlightened me. "She figured that it'd look like whoever killed Dunbar had run off with the books." He shook his head, amused with himself. "I'd sure love to tap her again. She was some firecracker."

I had heard enough. I didn't need details. I'd lived them. I punched him again, this time in the face. His nose matched that guy's in the movie *Chinatown*. The Barbarian slid down, hands to his face, whimpering about his broken beak.

I relaxed against the stall door, absorbed in what I had learned, when the door to the men's room opened and two other guys I'd never seen walked in with Mr. B behind them. He had come for the Barbarian's farewell party. Professional courtesy, I guess.

Chapter 20: Stakeout and Dinner

For half an hour I watched it. The BPD in unmarked cars. Two suits stood like Praetorian guards, one on each side of the front door. The unnamed citizen, Marty Savitz, had justified the protection detail and the Boston Police Department was more than willing to provide it. He knew and I knew that the BPD would riddle me dead before I made it to the station house. I watched the circus from a distance.

I was on the news. The photo of me they dredged up was less than flattering. The flyers were another joke at my expense. The safest place for me moving about Boston was below ground. The MBTA police were slow to cooperate because of the tedious rivalry between real cops and transit police. I had no interest in their fight. I was content to imitate Jean Valjean so long as I didn't run into Javert. I waited.

A hand touched my shoulder. "Hey, brother man."

"If it isn't the Tax Man himself," I answered.

I reached into my pocket for money for my Rastafarian friend with the guitar. His long black hands waved no. For a man of the streets, he was clean, almost too clean, and he didn't reek of alcohol, though I did detect a trace of weed. He reached into his pocket and pulled out my wanted poster, complete with phone number and substantial reward.

"Terrible picture of you," he said. He balled the paper up and did a hoop shot for the closest trash basket. He scored two points. "That office over yonder, the one the po-lice staked out…is them looking for you?"

I smiled. "Never understood why people pronounce the word that way."

"Cause we're trying to be po-lite."

"You're not calling the man, are you?"

He gave me a sideways look that could've punctured a tire.

"I don't think so," he said. "Way I figure it, them cats in blue are itching for an excuse to make you their scratching post." The street prophet had an apt metaphor. "You're looking for the lady secretary, aren't you?" His face brimmed with an incandescent smile that could've lit up the terminal end of the tunnel. "No hassle, man. Ms. Cummings is all right by me. Nice lady, if only she'd let her hair down." He shook a fist. I didn't know whether it meant "right on, and cool," or something obscene.

"You know her?" I asked. I had always thought street people would make the best detectives because they were invisible and they saw everything.

"Course I do. I know everybody in Kenmore Square, and they know me." He did a light bounce on his heels. He was proud of that fact.

"Everybody? Does that include cops?"

"They know of me, but don't know me. Not like I'm a vagrant and sit in one spot all day. Cops don't hassle you if you circulate and percolate." There was that bounce of pride again. "Sure, I may solicit here and there, but I offer folks a song and sometimes a hand, just like I'm helping you with a kind word, and not sending you over to Pontius Pilate."

I could've done without his allusion to judgment and crucifixion. "A helping hand, huh? Have you ever helped Ms. Cummings?"

"Sure, with bags and things, but mostly with a jingle on my gee-tar and a smile. She's down most of the time." His chin indicated why. "Her boss man isn't so nice."

"So I've learned. 'Bags and things'?"

"Carry them on down to the T-platform for her. I help her situate herself on the train."

"You don't have to answer if you don't want to, but what train does she take?"

"You do want to talk to her. Fox wants the hen."

"Nothing like that, but I doubt I'll talk to her with all these cops around."

"Sheesh, they protect the man. They have no interest in her. She clocks out a few minutes before five, so she can catch the B-train to Allston. She gets off at Washington Street and she always sits in the first car, if she can get the seat."

"Allston," I repeated.

"I know that look, brother, but I'm helping you so you can help her. Lady like that shouldn't be working for a crumb like him. I best go now. Peace."

I couldn't agree more. I watched him walk away. I called out to him and ironed out a Lincoln between my fingers. He laughed and said, "Save it for some other time when a brother is in need. How about that?"

"Deal. Hey, how about a name?"

"They call me Mr. Butch."

***

I anticipated her taking the Green Line by hopping into the first car one stop earlier at the Auditorium. My eyes checked the time on my wrist. The subway platform reminded me of the two sides of a confessional box, with Inbound on one side, Outbound on the other, and the metallic rails in between for a screen between penitent and priest.

I blended in with commuters as smoothly as brushed suede. I didn't look as hound-faced and tired as some of the office workers, but I kept my head down. The hard part—and it was always difficult—was finding a seat. Bostonians were born hockey players, the way they used their elbows and shoulders. The hesitant and polite were left to strap the ride and take the curves, the stutters and the gasps of the stops. At the Kenmore Square stop, commuters could disembark and choose the C-train for Cleveland Circle, or, two other trains that split to separate destinations: D for the bucolic trek to Riverside, or stay, like I did, on the B-train headed for Boston College.

Elizabeth Cummings boarded. A chivalric gent sacrificed his seat. I watched her do the rhythmic side-to-side or jerk in response to what the street and train dictated. Her stop, our stop, Washington Street, was the thirteenth one after Kenmore. I waited for Charlie Brown's teacher on the PA system to announce the stop.

She exited the first door, while I used the door in the middle of the trolley car. I held back to give her space. Please, no bus, I prayed. She walked two blocks to an apartment building. She pulled on a glass door that weighed

140

more than she did. I gave her time before I read the directory to locate her apartment.

I read names on brittle slips of paper next to the black buttons. She lived on the third floor. I did what impatient deliverymen do all the time. I pressed several buttons at once, hoping someone would buzz me, and it worked. The door unlatched. I was in.

My feet sandpapered dull marble steps. A thick banister offered some support against the incline. The cousins of the dead bugs from her office were present and accounted for. I found her door.

I rapped on the wood twice. The door advertised cracked paint and no peephole.

"Who is it?" the voice asked.

"Shane. Shane Cleary." I heard voices in the stairwell. I lowered my voice. "I'd like a word, please." No response. I tried a softer approach. "Elizabeth? It's me, Shane. Can we talk?"

I heard the chain slide and heard the links slap against the wood. The door opened. I spurted in and she closed the door fast.

"You have half the police force looking for you."

"Only half?"

I chained the door for her. Regret showed in her eyes. She backed away from me, hands knotted with worry. I had to reassure her and establish trust.

"I'm not going to hurt you. I just came here to talk. I wanted you to know I had nothing to do with what happened to Roger Sherman."

"What is it that you want from me?"

"Savitz. What can you tell me about him and hockey players? Are we talking strictly business, or something more?" I raised an eyebrow for nuance because I didn't want to get graphic and tell her about the sex club, the swing, and Bruin colors in Bay Village. When she didn't answer, I described the hockey player at the pinball machine.

She said nothing. She sat down and then shot up. She paced. Her living room was small enough to lay down one of those faded oval rugs and square enough for a modest table and a sofa. I conjectured that two people had to turn sideways in the bedroom, and the bathroom was a tight fit for both toilet and sink. She walked back and forth the way a parakeet wore out its perch.

"Relax, please."

"How can I relax? The police were at the office all day."

"For him, not you, and it'll stay that way," I said. She sat down like a good student.

I told her the protective detail will get pulled soon if nothing happened to Savitz. Her eyes lifted, wanting more of an explanation. "The department can't justify the expense, especially when there's a no-show, and I don't plan to visit the office. This hockey player of his—did Marty take a special interest in him?"

"Are you suggesting Marty is…?"

"Is he?"

"Not that I know of, but he did look after him."

"Like pay the tab at a certain bar?" She nodded. "Pay for transportation home?" Nod again. "Pay for anything else?" I got Bambi eyes this time. "You've got to tell me, Elizabeth. A man is already dead, and I'm not going down for a double murder." She hugged herself, but to the landlord's credit, it wasn't because the place was cold.

"Did you…did you kill that accountant?" she asked me.

"No, and I didn't kill Roger. Honest. A friend asked me to find Roger. Now, tell me, did Marty make any other kinds of payment?" She nodded, and I didn't like the shiver that accompanied it.

"He was paying Sherman," she said.

"For what?"

"Marty was getting these phone calls," she said. "Threatening kinds. I'd recognize the voice when the man called, and I'd patch it through to his office. It was Sherman. I never listened, but I heard Marty through the door more than once. He's quite vocal when he's upset."

"I can imagine. Anything else?"

"The hockey player's name was mentioned more than once."

"Then what?"

"Marty would have me prepare a cash envelope after one of those calls. A thousand, two thousand dollars at a time, and the amount kept going up."

"For how long?"

She shrugged, a look of defeat on her face. "I don't know: seven, maybe nine months. Marty didn't have the kind of clientele to support that kind of cash."

"This cash—where did you or Marty send it?"

"We didn't. A man would stop by and pick it up."

"And which part of all of this do you think Marty told the cops?"

"The threatening phone calls and you asking about Sherman, but he never mentioned the hockey player. I know because I could hear through the door."

"And the cops never spoke with you?"

"Not really. They ignored me and stuck with Marty, especially when he mentioned your name."

Her eyes got very serious, very scared. I stepped in closer to comfort her. I told her she was brave. I admired her for it. "This man who picked up the money. Did you get a good look at him?"

"I knew enough not to stare."

"Could you describe him to me?"

"He had a scar," she said and indicated where on his face. "Marty would write a number on the envelope and leave it on my desk after he took out money from the safe. He told me a man would stop by to pick it up."

"What kind of a number?"

"I have no idea." She recited the number. "Same number and same man every time."

I knew the scar. The number was short enough for a cop's badge. The dead Roger Sherman hired himself a bagman. Marty faced a PR-problem, just like Bray, except this one was about sex, the kind some people associated with ballet dancers and gymnasts, and not with blood and ice, the macho sport of hockey.

"I hate my job. I hate it," she said.

"I know you do. Most people hate their jobs."

"Do I have anything to worry about?"

"Marty doing all this in cash makes it hard to track, so the answer is no."

With what I knew about the number she'd written for Savitz on those envelopes, I wanted to tell her not to trust cops, but that would be a slap across the faces of all the men and women who wore the badge.

I felt her fingers in my shirt. I didn't want to look down into those brown eyes. She rested against me. "The police are after you, Shane."

"I'm used to it."

She pulled away and her chin lifted. I went in for the kiss; it was a soft one, a yielding and passionate one. I was in her tight arms. She moved and we moved and between kisses, she asked me if I would you stay for dinner. I said I would.

"Will you stay for more?"

"Think I already did."

Chapter 21: Friendly Fire

"It's never a quick, clean fight," I told myself in the mirror in the hallway in Brayton's townhouse. I checked the nasty contusion on my cheek, the leftover from my match with the Barbarian. The gash near my eye still smarted and my ribs ached something awful, though I don't recall the Barbarian landing punches. All in all, I felt like a typical Irishman after a long night at the pub, with more questions than answers.

In the ride over, words I'd practiced passed through my head. I'm no master of the subjunctive like Brando's Terry Malloy, but I've had my moments of wishful thinking. I had wished my father hadn't blown his brains out. I wished my mother had had a better life. I wished the professor had tenure. I wished it didn't matter what Bill did in the bedroom. I wished John didn't have to worry about the color of his skin. I wished cops were as virtuous and upstanding as Joe Friday. I wished for a lot of things.

"Mr. Braddock will see you now," the butler told me. We repeated the routine. We traveled the same train tracks as the first night I'd visited the lord and lady of the house. The difference this time was that it was morning and I'd taken a cab. He opened the door and announced me. A first.

"You should've called. We could've had breakfast together," Brayton said.

"I should have called, yes. Where is Cat?"

"Is this about the case?"

"It is," I said. I put my hands behind my back. "Please call her."

Brayton instructed the butler to call Mrs. Braddock on her line. I waited, taking in the familiar room. The fireplace wasn't lit. The small bar and studded bottle of brandy was still there, as was the rotary phone.

It rang moments after the butler left.

"There she is," he said. He let it ring, which confused me and Bray took the moment to educate me. "When I don't answer it, she'll come downstairs. You wanted to speak to her?"

"To both of you, actually," I said.

"About the case?"

I dislike repeating myself. I said nothing and stood there like a good soldier at ease in the thick of an awkward silence. Brayton was no master of small talk and I had no interest in hearing about the terrible acoustics at the symphony, or his disappointment with the view from his box at the opera. He offered me a drink. Too early in the morning, I said, but I advised him to pour His and Her drinks. I heard footsteps and the door open.

"Shane has news for us, dear."

"Hello, Shane. This is a pleasant surprise." Cat placed her kiss under the Barbarian's signature on my cheek. "That's gotta hurt." She touched it. I winced. "So, what's this news?"

"Take your drink and sit down, please. The same goes for you, Bray."

Cat accepted her drink from him. She sat down in one of the armchairs. Brayton poured himself a generous splash and took his chair.

"You were right, Bray. You were being blackmailed."

"What did I tell you!" he said with his snifter and glanced over at Cat. "That Dunbar had a lot of gall to ask for fifty-thousand dollars per page."

"About that, Bray," I said. "Tell me exactly how you found out your blackmailer wanted fifty K per page. I'm curious."

"My wife told me."

Brayton had that puzzled look this side of stupid, like when people are one letter short of the crossword clue, and all the other surrounding squares are filled in and they still can't make out the word.

"Cat told you, correct?"

"She did. Why, is it important?"

"Very, I'm afraid. She told me the same thing. How did she tell you?"

"How? Over the telephone. She said she received a phone call."

"Really?" I said. "She told me the same thing, but it wasn't over the phone."

I put my hands into my pockets. I did that slow-walk the detectives do in the movies to make people sweat. Columbo did it, and I imagined Marlowe did it. I know Spade did. Cat and I looked at each other. Her expression was colder than the marbled fireplace.

Brayton glanced at her and then at me. "When did she tell you?"

"After," I said.

"After what?"

I parked myself in front of Cat. "Should I tell him or you?"

"Is that really necessary?" she asked.

"No, it isn't."

I moved and stood in front of Brayton.

"The telephone is a popular means of communication these days. Hard to keep all those numbers straight. Perhaps the caller used one of these," I said to him as I pulled out the business card from my pocket. "I found it next to me the night your driver brought me here."

Brayton examined the card, turned it over and saw the handwritten phone number. Cat sat there, snifter in hand. She took a sip. Lucrezia Borgia couldn't have done it more delicately.

He looked to her in disbelief and said, "This is my card, but why is your phone number on the back? This isn't your handwriting." His thumb passed over the inked numbers. Cat didn't answer.

"An excellent question, Bray, and you're right, it's not her writing," I said.

Cat wasn't one for drama. She was never one for a sudden confession, or a burst of tears. She sat there like an iceberg.

"Tell me, Bray," I said. "Isn't it odd that out of the hundreds of people who work for you, out of all the buildings and floors you own in Boston, Dunbar the consultant was miraculously your man?"

Bray's thumb raked the edge of the business card. A Trappist monk would've broken his vow of silence, demanded an explanation or something. Not Brayton Braddock III.

"Here's what I think," I said, my lips not far from his ear. "I think you convinced yourself it was Dunbar after your wife planted his name in your mind. Perhaps she whispered it into your ear, like I'm doing now. She suggested him to you, like she recommended me for this case, didn't she?"

His eyes read the front and back of the card in his hand. His other hand held his snifter, giving the precious nectar a slight twirl.

"There were photocopies," he said in a low voice. "You saw them."

"I did. Here's where you can plug that smug nickel you fed me about how it was common practice to keep two ledgers in the wonderful and magical world of finance. Remember the night of the party? Same night Dunbar was murdered."

I decided to pace the carpet again.

"You were right about one thing the night you hired me: exposure would've sunk the deal, given you and your cronies a bad rash, the kind of PR that's gets nasty with unpleasant questions from an auditor." I snapped my fingers to jar him. "And just like that I'm on the case. You knew I needed the money, didn't you? Only problem in all of this mess is your wife knew more than she let on. The question is, how did she know?"

Cat took a hot gulp of brandy. I looked over and asked her, "How am I doing, Cat?"

"What the hell are you getting at?" Brayton said, up on his feet in faux outrage.

"Park it, brother. Sit down on your little throne there because she's made an idiot out of you, and you're making a fool of yourself now. See, Cat understood mobsters were wired into this deal. She knew dealing with the mob was the cost of doing business, with construction, labor unions and all."

I lifted my chin to indicate Cat. "She picked herself a gangster out of the litter, a real bruiser. Here's a dose of irony for you, Bray. He was illiterate. He wouldn't have been able to read your name on the front of that calling card in your hand, Bray, but boy, did he know numbers." I walked over to stand in front of Cat again. "You met him at the Copley Square Hotel, isn't that right, Cat? That's where you two made a little noise and hatched a deal."

"Deal?" Bray wrenched his head left to look at his wife. "Hotel?"

"Interesting word choice there, Bray. 'Deal' bolts to the forefront of your little brain instead of 'hotel' and the idea of your wife there with a dangerous man?" The surprise in my own voice was genuine. "The deal was to sink

148

you and the real estate project. She paid her gangster fifty grand to find your books and make copies of them. She used those copies to convince you that you were being blackmailed."

Brayton didn't look at me, nor did he look at her. I spared her hubby the replay of her as Lana Turner and the Barbarian as Johnny Stompanato. He fussed with his card, his brandy. The vein in his temple throbbed. He stewed there like a pot of steamers. I had more for him.

"Your sweetheart of a wife wanted out of her marriage to you. You'd become a pariah, if the real estate deal went south, and people went down with you. She'd divorce you and take you for everything you're worth. And, if any suits darkened her door with questions, she'd feign ignorance because business is men's work, but something went terribly wrong. Didn't it, Cat?"

I saw her profile. Her eyelashes didn't move.

"Will you tell him, Cat, or should I?"

After another sip she said, "You're talking nonsense, a ridiculous fairy tale."

"Am I?" I said. "The interesting thing about fairy tales is that they have scary monsters and surprise endings. Our story has a creature named the Barbarian and an unexpected surprise."

"Who's the Barbarian?" Bray asked.

"He's the guy I said earlier who was dangerous and illiterate, but good with numbers. He's the guy she met at the Copley Hotel. He's the gangster who saw trouble when he learned about Dunbar. The question is how did he learn about the murdered accountant? I'll tell you. See, when you're on the run from the cops like I've been, you learn a lot about the darker side of the street. You find friends in unexpected places. Enemies become friends and friends become enemies. With me so far, Bray?"

"No, and what's Dunbar have to do with my wife?"

"I'll get to that," I said. "But a question first. Did you know that some mobsters are government informants? Dunbar let me in on that tidbit when he told me the government had moles inside organized crime. I didn't put the pieces together right away until I asked myself one curious question, How does a psychotic, like the Barbarian, get away with outrageous crimes and avoid hard time? Like I said, enemies become allies. Are you following me,

Brayton?"

"Not exactly."

"The Barbarian was an informant. When he found out Dunbar was going through your books, he told your wife, and that's how you got Dunbar's name, my friend."

Cat sat cool as a snowflake.

My ear itched and I scratched it. "There's one detail the Barbarian didn't share with your wife, though."

Her head turned then. I saw worry lines.

"Dunbar was FBI." I crossed my arms like a disgusted schoolteacher. "Dunbar was an auditor with a shield. Quirky fellow, sort of weird, and I didn't like him at first, but he grew on me once I started talking to him. I learned from him how the government can't make laws fast enough to keep up with men in business suits, and how you and the Mayflower crowd are no different than any of the mafia families. Only the names are different. I've got to hand it to her, Bray. She almost pulled it off."

I ran my hand over the top of Brayton's armchair. Nice material.

"Dunbar told me he was FBI the night he died. Why? I was persona non grata. Who would believe me? I think he was trying to warn me, tell me what I was up against before he was clipped. I got knocked out and woke up to his dead body. Luck of the Irish for me there. I began to think set-up, and me as the patsy. The entire Boston Police Department bumped my name to the top of the wanted list. I suspect neither of you would've lost any sleep if something had happened to me. Don't worry, I don't take it personal. You two have enough problems. A dead auditor is murder, and cooked books are fraud. The DA's office can sort out the rest of the charges."

Cat leapt up. "You have no proof. None."

Bray joined in for the chorus. "You have nothing but a theory."

"That's where you're wrong." I shook my head. "The two of you are really something. You both sat back, all comfortable in your chairs with your fancy grape juice when it shaped up like I would be taking the fall for Dunbar's murder, except I didn't kill him and neither did the Barbarian."

Cat's face dropped.

"That's right, he didn't kill the accountant. The man was right for the part. I almost watched that movie myself."

They both looked like mannequins in a store window.

"The Barbarian was certifiable—no argument there, but he wouldn't jeopardize whatever deal he had with the Feds by killing a shield. Sure, the government let him commit crimes because they were getting something in return from him, but they'd draw a line through his name if he murdered one of their own. Dunbar dead left you in a predicament, didn't it, Cat?"

"I don't know what you're talking about."

"Yes, you do. A dead federal auditor is asking for a swarm of accountants hell-bent on those ledgers and justice for their colleague. You convinced your husband he's being blackmailed; that required copies of the ledgers, but when Dunbar was killed you asked your boyfriend the gangster to collect whatever ledgers he could find in the Little Building. Unfortunately for you and him, he ran into me, and I got to the ledgers first."

Cat had kept her package together through all of this, but I could see she was starting to fray. She was breathing fast. I touched her shoulder.

"I honestly believe you didn't want to see me get hurt, and you thought it was clear sailing, until Dunbar was murdered and you found out from the papers that he was a Fed. Me framed-up for murder would make life easier for everyone, and…"

"Don't believe him, Bray," Cat said. "He doesn't know what he's talking about."

Brayton stood up again. "Then who killed Dunbar?"

"Your driver did," I said.

"Absurd," she said.

"Is it? He's loyal as a dog, remember? He was there in the car when the Barbarian told you about Dunbar. The rest is history."

Cat clenched her jaw. If her hair had moved, I would've thought she was the Medusa. Her words came, slow as an icicle melted. "Are you implying I instructed him to kill Dunbar?"

"I'm not implying that at all. Perhaps, he took it upon himself to talk to Dunbar, persuade him to hand over the books, or tell him where the originals were kept. Perhaps, he had no intention of killing Dunbar. I'd like to think he didn't want to murder the man."

"And what makes you arrive at the conclusion?" she asked me.

"Because he killed Dunbar with my gun, which suggests he arrived unarmed. Like you, he didn't know Dunbar was federal. Like you, he didn't expect to find me there. I can't say what went through his mind because I was knocked unconscious."

Bray slid down a little in his chair, speechless. Cat lowered herself into her chair, as if she were to become ill. I could see it in their eyes. The king and queen had realized their little kingdom was close to the sea, too close and could get washed away. Brayton kicked back the last of the brandy.

"Is that all?" Bray asked.

"No, I'm afraid not. My friend Bill, the cop, has your driver down at the station. Who knows what he'll say? Your driver might be loyal and obedient and take the rap for everything, or he can sit closed like an Ipswich clam, but I wouldn't underestimate the BPD. They can get a blind man to confess to what he saw last night. He might mention the Barbarian. He might not. Who knows. As for the Barbarian, he's on a plane to San Francisco, and I don't think anyone will hear from him again, if ever, which may work in your favor. As for ledgers, they're with an Italian in the North End, and you'll need more than your family name and influence if you want them back."

Bray snapped, "Those are my property."

"And I need the insurance should anything happen to me."

"They'll never put us away," Brayton said, smug as a bedbug.

"You're probably right. You people pay for laws to be written and torn down, not unlike buildings in this town. Most of you have law degrees, which makes it worse. Spend enough money, and you'll get the justice you can afford. One thing is certain, though: you have to live with each other."

The doorbell buzzed. The surprise jolted Bray.

"Those are the cops, and they have warrants. Let the butler get the door, Bray. The two of you should finish your brandy. Henri IV Heritage, aged in oak for a century. You don't know when you'll enjoy the pleasure again. Shame for it to go unappreciated."

Brayton turned to Cat. "You wanted to ruin me. Why?"

Cat didn't move. She held her snifter.

"Answer me! I want to know why."

"Maybe I can answer that for you."

Bray glared at me. "Haven't you said enough?"

"Think back to the night of your shindig. The brunette you and your friends circled and drooled over. 'Bray's latest flavor, and for more than a month' is how your wife described her to me."

His face relaxed. "Don't be ridiculous."

"A real looker," I said. "She's a mathematician, a potential Wall Street wizard, someone who can make you money, someone who brings her own to the table, which is something Cat can't do. She's someone who can replace your wife when her looks have faded."

Cat turned her head away. I'd wounded her. I moved in on Bray.

"A girl like Cat is like a stock. It's all about what's printed on the paper and the value people assign it that determines her worth. I know your wife, Bray. You think you know her, but you don't. I heard her voice that night, and nothing is more terrifying than being vulnerable or the fear of not being wanted. Trust me, I'm acquainted with those feelings well, and they don't wear well."

Bray left the room.

We were alone. The ceilings were still high; the carpet illustrated the allegory of the hunt. I stood on the figure of a speared boar.

Cat stood up. "I thought you loved me."

"I did. You taught me a kiss doesn't mean love. I got thrown over for Bray, and I didn't like it. I had neither money nor the pedigree. I hated you for that. Then, I disliked you for a long time, but when I saw you again I'll admit I got caught up in the nostalgia. But that's no longer a problem for me. The past is the past and belongs there."

"I didn't mean for you to get hurt. I do care."

"I'd like to believe that," I said.

Her lips moved to gather moisture. I raised her chin for one last look.

"You care in your way, but that isn't love. Survival and comfort, security and the nice things in life are more important to you. If love meant so much to you, you could've walked out of this house a long time ago and not given a damn about palaces and bank accounts. You didn't. Dunbar loved his job and it got him killed. I love my job and you almost got me killed. There should be justice for a man killed on the job he loves. I'm doing this for the crummy auditor married to his desk. He was somebody and you made him nobody."

Chapter 22: Closing Shop

Jimmy turned his head when he heard the tinkle of the bell. I found him behind the counter detailing the shutters of a dollhouse. He set aside the small brush, and lifted the special bifocals up. He looked at me and I looked at him.

"Sorry about your friend Roger," I said, placing the developed roll of film on the counter. Jimmy considered it, but said nothing. I nudged it forward. His fingers accepted it.

"Looks like Kodak film," he said.

"Color of the box reminds me of the Bruins." I pointed to the sealed envelope. "A friend of mine, who is very discreet, developed the roll for me. You've got my word nobody else knows. The negatives are inside the envelope. Do what you will with them."

The man had lost a friend and saved my life. I hadn't gotten to his friend in time, but we both knew the game that Roger was playing came with consequences. Jimmy unpeeled the adhesive lip and let the small packet of photos slide out. The negatives slipped out like loose change. I had to tell Jimmy.

"He was blackmailing a sports agent, and the agent had to protect his purse. This wouldn't have ended well for Roger. You have to know that, Jimmy. If the agent hadn't gotten to him, then the mob would've eventually shut him down, for the same reason. Money always talks and blackmail hurts business."

He shook his head as he examined the pictures. His jaw tightened. "Maybe I could've stopped him if I had known."

155

"Don't do that to yourself."

"He was my friend and I loved him once."

"I know, but some people you can't save. I know you don't want to hear that, Jimmy, but it's the truth."

He wiped away a tear from the corner of his eye. "This agent, this guy Savitz, what happens to him?"

"Nothing, on account of a lack of evidence."

"I see," he said and held out his hand. We shook hands. I looked at the dollhouse. Never understood the hobby, but it required concentration, a lot of effort to place everything where it belonged inside. Some people live their entire lives like that, with everything just right, not knowing how small they are until someone rips the roof off.

I saw the fedora under the glass. "How much for the hat?" I asked Jimmy.

"I knew you'd come back for it," Jimmy said. He reached under the counter. The glare of the light reminded me how large his hand was, how he kept his fingernails manicured. He handed me the fedora.

"Let's see whether it fits," I said.

The hat and I were made for each other. I ran my fingers around the brim.

"It fits. You could pass for Marlowe."

"Afraid I'm not as idealistic," I said.

"This town could use a dreamer."

"How much do I owe you?" I asked as I reached into my pocket.

"On the house."

I walked out of Jimmy's nostalgia shop into a dark overcast Boston day a different man, one who could find the sun in the sky and accept that it didn't have to shine bright every day.

***

Sylvia stuffed us with her food. The moment I walked into the room, a mélange of scents and spices greeted me. She had numerous pots and saucepans over flames. A mirepoix of equal parts chopped celery, carrots, and onions was ready to join garlic cloves and bay leaves for braised short ribs with seared shrimp and grits. She slapped my hand away when I tried to peel away the aluminum foil to peek inside a tray. I had glimpsed grilled corn cobs. I exacted a pinch of freshly grated Cotija cheese on a small dish as a tribute.

I inquired about an Irish familiar, the potatoes she had on the counter. I pointed to her wall. There, she had mounted a medieval device that transformed spuds into fries, but that was not the fate she planned for these tubers my tribe had loved and abandoned in Ireland. She showed me a grater and the cloth that she would use to squeeze out all the water so she could make a potato hash.

Sylvia expelled me from her kitchen after I'd tried to sample her pièce de résistance: a bacon apple crisp that had been cooling in a skillet on a trivet on her window sill. I'd do hard time in solitary confinement for one bite. I asked if she'd serve it with vanilla ice cream, and almost wept when she told me about the salted bourbon caramel she made to accompany the dessert.

We ate well that night. My eyes did a lap of gratitude around the table. Sylvia and I were good. She hadn't thanked me outright for bringing John home safe, but I received a generous helping of pork butt with the most perfect bark after she said Grace. We talked like a family, and I had not had that pleasure for a long time.

Bill mentioned the date for his detective's exam. I glanced at the professor. He raised his glass and I raised mine. Delano Lindsey didn't have a permanent job, but the agency said his current gig was guaranteed for six more weeks.

We ignored the news. The newspapers had spent a lot of dark ink on the Braddocks, the real estate imbroglio, but we didn't pay any attention to it. We ate and we drank and made merry. The waterfront deal and any talk about an artery was on the back burner. When people forgot—and they would—the map of the waterfront would get rolled out again, like fresh carpet, when it suited the wealthy in this town.

Brayton and Cat would beat the rap. Odds were in their favor that a battalion of lawyers would either clear them of malfeasance or bargain the charges against them down to a blush. There was the other possibility: their driver. He could take an extended vacation for them in Walpole. When he got out, he'd find a number and several zeroes after it in a bank account in the Canary Islands. Papa Hemingway was right about the rich: they are different because they have more money.

Bray and Cat had each other and in my eyes that was punishment enough.

I thought about Elizabeth Cummings in the front car on the Allston-bound train tonight. Mr. Butch would have a song for her and for all those passing through Kenmore tonight and tomorrow.

Then there's that cop with a scar I met at the late Roger Sherman's house. He didn't get his but I had his badge number and we would meet again under a different moon. I know that for certain because this is a small town.

John taxied the Professor to Cambridge, Bill to Bay Village, and me back home in Union Park in the South End. I had cash to my name. The landlord and I were on good terms again. Business, not personal, she said, and I teased her. She had seen *The Godfather*. No hard feelings, I assured her. Christmas had come late, but it came, and I had 1976 ahead of me.

It's a hard, cold January now, with Valentine hearts in the shop windows and plans in the air for a festive July and The Spirit of '76.

I climbed my stairs. I had my keys, my door, and a place I called home. I had my girl at my feet and next to me in bed. We had made up, or at least Delilah allowed me the illusion that all was forgiven. I doubted it. I doubt a lot of things, except that Boston is Boston.

My town, this dirty old town.

Acknowledgements

I'm indebted to **Dave King**, who read the first draft of *Dirty Old Town* in 2015. He offered criticism and encouragement, for which I'm grateful for a better story. **Dean Hunt** has proofed all my work over the years and his careful eyes have saved me countless times from foolish errors. **Deb Well** and **Kimberly Stieglitz** have acted as my beta readers and provided me with suggestions and memorable conversations. **Shawn Reilly Simmons**, an accomplished author, worked with me through developmental edits and final edits. Her suggestions, like a chef's instinct for flavor at the right time, helped me improve the story. I'm grateful to **Level Best Books** who has given the Shane Cleary stories a home. Thank you, one and all.

About the Author

Gabriel Valjan lives in Boston's South where he enjoys the local restaurants. When he isn't appeasing Squeak, his cat and editor, with turkey, he documents the #dogsofsouthendboston on Instagram. His short stories have appeared online, in journals, and in several anthologies. He has been a finalist for the Fish Prize, shortlisted for the Bridport Prize, and received an Honorable Mention for the Nero Wolfe Black Orchid Novella Contest. Gabriel is the author of two series, *Roma* and *Company Files*, with Winter Goose Publishing. *Dirty Old Town* is the first in the Shane Cleary series for Level Best Books. You can find him on Twitter (@GValjan) and Instagram (gabrielvaljan). He lurks the hotel hallways at crime fiction conferences, such as Bouchercon, Malice Domestic, and New England Crime Bake. Gabriel is a lifetime member of Sisters in Crime.

CPSIA information can be obtained
at www.ICGtesting.com
Printed in the USA
BVHW031956150222
629110BV00013B/99